This book belongs to:

....

CONTENTS

STORIES BY IAN ROBINSON
ILLUSTRATED BY JOHN HARROLD
STORY COLOURING BY GINA HART

John Harrold.

RUPERT

John Harrold.

THE EXPRESS ANNUAL

Pedigree®
BOOKS

Published by Pedigree Books Limited
The Old Rectory, Matford Lane, Exeter, EX2 4PS.

No 62

£6.99
RU62

RUPERT and

*One day Rupert sets out to try
A model plane he wants to fly . . .*

One day, Rupert decides to fly his model plane on Nutwood Common. As he sets out, he suddenly notices something odd. "There's no birdsong!" he murmurs. "The birds are flying about without making a sound." Just then, Rupert's chum Edward comes running towards him. He is in such a hurry that he doesn't seem to notice there is anyone there . . . "Hello!" calls Rupert. "What's the matter? Where are you off to in such a rush?"

the Song Snatcher

*"There's Edward Trunk, but where can he
Be running to so hurriedly?"*

*"My mother's ill – she's strained her throat
And cannot sing a single note!"*

When Edward sees Rupert, he stops to explain that he is on his way to fetch the doctor . . . "My mother suddenly lost her voice!" he declares. "She wants Dr. Lion to come and see her straightaway." "I saw his car on my way here," says Rupert. "He'd just stopped outside Bill's house." "Thanks, Rupert!" says Edward. "I'd better be on my way." "I'll come too!" says Rupert. "If Dr. Lion isn't at Bill's, I'll be able to help you look for him . . ."

*"The doctor's gone to visit Bill –
I think that Mrs. Badger's ill . . ."*

RUPERT VISITS MRS. TRUNK

"Hello!" says Dr. Lion. "I see . . .
You two had better come with me!"

The doctor tells the two chums how
Bill's mother can't sing either now.

"So, Mrs. Trunk! Your throat's sore too!
Let's see what I can do for you."

"It's very strange! I tried to sing
But Pompey couldn't hear a thing!"

The pals arrive at Bill's house just as Dr. Lion is leaving. When he hears what is wrong he agrees to make Edward's house his next call. "You two can come with me," he says. "You've already had a long walk and it won't take a moment in the car . . ." As they drive along, Dr. Lion tells the pair that Bill's mother has lost her voice too. "It's very strange!" he declares. "She was sitting near the window, singing a lullaby to Baby Badger, when she suddenly found she couldn't sing another note!"

"Thank goodness you're here!" gasps Mrs. Trunk as Dr. Lion arrives. "I don't know what's wrong. I've never known anything like it!" "Tell me what happened," says the doctor. "It was on the Common," explains Edward's mother. "I'd taken young Pompey out for a walk and was singing him some nursery rhymes as we went along . . . All of a sudden, I couldn't sing another note!" "Very strange!" agrees Dr. Lion. "Perhaps this linctus will do the trick . . ."

RUPERT HEARS A CALL

The doctor says he'll call again.
"I hope your mother's better then!"

"It does sound odd!" says Mrs. Bear.
"There must be something in the air!"

Next morning Mrs. Badger still
Can't sing but says, "I don't feel ill!"

As Rupert goes to Edward's he
Hears someone calling, from a tree . . .

"I hope your mother feels better tomorrow," says Rupert as the doctor drives away. "I expect so," says Edward. "The funny thing is, she can speak but can't sing . . ." Later that evening, as Rupert gets ready for bed, he tells his parents what has happened. "It does seem peculiar that two people should lose their voices," agrees Mrs. Bear. "I wonder what's the matter?" "Probably some sort of bug!" declares Rupert's father. "A spoonful of linctus should put them both right again . . ."

Next morning, Rupert goes to Bill's house to see if his mother is any better . . . "I feel fine," declares Mrs. Badger. "But I still can't sing a note! "I wonder if Mrs. Trunk is better yet?" thinks Rupert. He hurries across the Common to visit Edward. Rupert hasn't gone far when he suddenly hears someone call his name. "Come here!" hoots the Wise Old Owl. "There's something very strange going on and I need your help to get to the bottom of it!"

RUPERT DISCOVERS A MYSTERY

The Wise Old Owl says something's wrong –
"Each Nutwood bird has lost its song!"

"They try to sing but, as you see,
Their beaks just open silently."

Then Horace Hedgehog comes to tell
How he's found something odd as well . . .

"It's hidden in the long grass where
Nobody else can see it there!"

Rupert is surprised to hear that the Wise Old Owl is puzzled. "Normally it's the other way round," he says. "Everyone comes to you to find out what has been happening . . ." "I know what has been happening," says the owl. "The thing is, I don't know why!" Pointing with his wing, he tells Rupert that lots of Nutwood's birds have suddenly lost their voices. "Can't sing a note!" he declares. "That's just what happened to Mrs. Trunk!" gasps Rupert. "She lost her voice, too . . ."

As Rupert speaks, he hears a rustling sound from somewhere nearby. "Horace!" he cries. "Fancy meeting you! I thought you didn't come out much during the day." "I don't!" says the little hedgehog. "But I heard you both talking and came to see what's happening." When he learns how the birds have lost their songs, Horace looks thoughtful – then tells Rupert to come and see something strange. "It's just by the edge of the Common," he explains. "I found it hidden in the long grass . . ."

RUPERT FINDS A MACHINE

Rupert kneels down, amazed to find
A tiny machine of some kind . . .

"How strange! Whatever could it be?
I think I'll take it home with me . . ."

"What's that?" asks Mr. Bear. "I say!
A gramophone! Does it still play?"

A song begins. "I recognise
That voice – Bill's mother!" Rupert cries.

When they reach the edge of the Common, Rupert kneels down to see what Horace has found. Peering into a clearing, he spots a strange device, hidden in the bushes. "What is it?" asks Horace. I don't know," says Rupert, picking up the machine for a closer look. "It reminds me of something but I can't remember what . . ." "Do you think it's got anything to do with the missing birdsongs?" whispers his friend. "It might," agrees Rupert. "I'll take it home to show Mum and Dad . . ."

When Rupert arrives home, his parents are both outside. "Hello," says Mrs. Bear. "Whatever's that you're carrying?" "I don't know," says Rupert. "I found it up on the Common . . ." "It looks like an old-fashioned gramophone!" declares Rupert's father. "Although it's smaller than the ones I remember."As he examines Rupert's find, Mr. Bear pushes a lever which makes the machine start playing. "A nursery rhyme!" cries Rupert. "I recognise that voice! It's Bill's mother!"

RUPERT AND BILL LOOK FOR MORE

*Next morning, Rupert goes to find
If more machines are left behind . . .*

*Bill Badger runs to tell him how
His mother's song has come back now!*

*As soon as Bill hears Rupert's quest
He joins in, searching for the rest . . .*

*Just as they find one, someone comes
Marching towards the startled chums!*

Next morning, Rupert decides to see if there are any more of the strange devices hidden on the Common. As he sets off, he hears someone calling, then spots Bill Badger hurrying towards him. "Hello!" smiles his chum. "I was just on my way to tell you the news. My mother's got her voice back!" "You mean she can sing again?" asks Rupert. "That's right!" laughs Bill. "It happened yesterday, as we were having tea . . ." "Gosh!" says Rupert. "Just when the machine I found started to play!"

"What machine?" blinks Bill. As soon as he hears Rupert's story, he agrees to help search the Common to see if there are any more. "Do you think they can really capture songs?" he asks. "I don't know," says Rupert. "But it might explain why all the birds have suddenly stopped singing." The pair look everywhere until they reach a stand of trees by the edge of the wood. "Here's one!" cries Rupert. "I wonder who . . ." "Look out!" calls Bill. "Somebody's coming!"

RUPERT'S PAL SPOTS A STRANGER

"Who's that?" asks Bill. "He's searching too!
Let's see what he decides to do . . ."

Not realising he's been seen,
The man picks up the last machine.

"Wait!" Rupert calls. "Please tell me what
You do with those machines you've got . . ."

The man walks forward silently –
"He's clockwork! Look, Bill! There's his key!"

The two pals take cover behind a tree as the stranger approaches. "What odd clothes!" whispers Bill. "I wonder where he's from?" The little man is pulling a handcart piled high with the strange machines. "He must be collecting them from all over the Common!" gasps Rupert. Sure enough, the stranger stops as he reaches the clearing and picks up the machine that Rupert has just found. Carrying it over to the handcart, he nods stiffly then loads it aboard.

Determined to discover what's going on, Rupert steps out from behind the tree and calls to the stranger. "Who are you?" he asks. "Why have you hidden machines all over Nutwood Common?" To the chums' surprise, the little man doesn't say a word. Ignoring them completely, he starts forward with the handcart as if nobody was there . . . "Look!" cries Rupert. "He's a clockwork doll!" "You're right!" gasps Bill. "But where's he come from? Let's follow him and see where he goes . . ."

13

RUPERT SEES A FLYING BOAT

The pals pursue the clockwork man.
"We've got to stop him if we can!"

They stand amazed by what they see –
"A flying boat!" blinks Bill. "Bless me!"

"Stop!" Rupert cries. "You mustn't take
The songs our birds are meant to make!"

The clockwork man ignores his call,
As though there's no-one there at all!

The two pals hurry after the little man, who marches more briskly now that he has gathered up the last machine. Before long they reach a grassy clearing where an extraordinary sight meets their astonished gaze . . . "It's some sort of flying boat!" whispers Bill. As the pair look on, the little man lowers a special ramp and begins to wheel his trolley aboard. "Quick, Bill!" cries Rupert. "We mustn't let him get away! Those machines have stolen songs from half the birds in Nutwood . . ."

"Stop!" cries Rupert, running towards the balloon. Luckily, he reaches the ramp just in time to clamber aboard. "Who sent you here?" he asks the little man. "Why have you stolen so many songs?" The stranger gives no answer but turns silently to the airship's controls. "Wait!" calls Rupert. "You can't go yet . . ." The man pushes a lever forward and the ramp begins to close. "I've got to stop him!" thinks Rupert. "If we don't get those machines back, the stolen songs will disappear!"

RUPERT IS CARRIED OFF

The ramp shuts. Rupert looks around.
The boat starts rising from the ground!

"Jump!" Bill calls, but the boat's too high –
It drifts off, up into the sky . . .

"Come back!" calls Bill, but it's too late.
The clockwork pilot doesn't wait.

He steers a course and off they go,
Soon leaving Nutwood far below . . .

Before Rupert can do anything, the ramp of the airship snaps shut with a loud click. The little man pulls a second lever and the boat begins to rise. "We're taking off!" gasps Rupert. He pushes at the ramp as hard as he can only to find that it is impossible to open . . . "Jump!" calls Bill, but the airship is already too high. Rupert hears the whirr of a propeller and feels the boat surge forward. The clockwork figure turns the ship's wheel, then stares blankly ahead . . .

"Come back!" cries Bill, running after the flying boat as fast as he can, but it's too late! Leaving him far behind, it rises higher and higher, until Rupert can see the whole of Nutwood, like a giant model village. "Where are we going?" he asks anxiously. The little man says nothing, but stands stiffly at the ship's wheel, steering a steady course. "I'd forgotten he's only clockwork!" thinks Rupert. "I suppose he's been given orders to fly straight home."

RUPERT ARRIVES AT A CASTLE

The boat flies on until it nears
A mountain peak which disappears . . .

What happens next is a surprise –
The balloon swells. They start to rise!

"A gleaming palace!" Rupert blinks.
"It's hidden out of sight," he thinks.

The clockwork pilot seems to know
Exactly where he has to go . . .

Driven along by its whirring propeller, the airship leaves Nutwood and travels over far-off fields and forests. As Rupert peers over the pilot's shoulder he sees a rocky mountain appear on the horizon, so tall that its peak is hidden in a thick layer of cloud. To his surprise, the little man steers directly towards it. As they draw near, the balloon swells with a sudden hiss of gas and they start to climb even higher. The next moment, the ship is completely engulfed in swirling clouds . . .

For a few moments all Rupert can see is billowing mist, then the airship emerges above the clouds in a glow of golden sunshine. Directly ahead lies the top of the mountain, with an extraordinary castle set on its summit. "It's completely hidden by clouds!" gasps Rupert. "From down below, nobody would ever know it was here . . ." The little man pulls a lever and they begin to lose height. Sailing over the ramparts, he steers down towards the open courtyard.

RUPERT GOES INSIDE

Two sentries guard the Palace gate –
They shoulder arms and stand quite straight.

"They're clockwork!" Rupert gasps. "I see –
Each soldier has a little key!"

Inside the palace, Rupert's sure
He'll find out who the songs are for . . .

He wanders through a great hall. "There
Are clockwork figures everywhere!"

As the flying boat clears the castle walls, Rupert spots two sentries. To his surprise, they show no interest in the boat, but stand stiffly to attention, staring straight ahead . . . The little man lowers the ship's ramp and starts to unload the machines. "I wonder where he's taking them now?" thinks Rupert. As nobody seems to have noticed him, he decides to follow the man inside. It is only when he reaches the sentries that Rupert suddenly realises that they are clockwork too . . .

Following the little man inside the castle, Rupert finds himself at the foot of an ornate staircase. "It's like a palace!" he marvels. The man climbs briskly to the top of the stairs, then marches off to another room. When Rupert reaches the doorway, he is utterly astonished at what lies inside. There before him stand clockwork figures of every shape and size: animals, acrobats, conjurers and clowns . . . "Amazing!" blinks Rupert. "It must be the biggest collection in the world!"

RUPERT IS DISCOVERED

The little man still hurries on
But Rupert soon spots where he's gone . . .

He climbs the stairs and doesn't stop
Until he's reached the very top.

Inside the room an old man beams –
The songs are all for him, it seems . . .

He jumps up with a start. "Who's there?
Good gracious! It's a little bear!"

Rupert is so fascinated by the marvellous collection of toys that he hardly notices the little man disappear through a set of curtains at the far end of the room. Hurrying towards them, Rupert is just in time to see him, climbing yet another flight of stairs. This time the steps lead to the top of a tall tower, where the man pushes open a little door. "Come in!" cries a voice. "About time too! I hope you've managed to gather all the songs I asked for. There really isn't a moment to lose . . ."

Overcome with curiosity, Rupert climbs to the top of the stairs and peers inside the room. The little man stands motionless before an elderly figure, seated at a cluttered work-bench. "Nutwood songs!" he smiles, gazing at the recording machines. "We've never had any from there before . . ." Suddenly, he notices Rupert standing in the doorway and breaks off with a cry of surprise. "Who are you?" he asks incredulously. "What do you want? However did you get here?"

RUPERT SEES A TOY BIRD

"Your clockwork servant brought me when
He flew home in his boat again."

"Young Wolfgang's a great help to me.
I make new clockwork toys, you see . . ."

"He fetches back the songs he's heard,
For musical toys, like this bird."

The toy bird starts to flap its wings,
Then, like a real one, sings and sings . . .

When Rupert explains he has come from Nutwood, the old man seems astonished. "I saw your servant collecting the recording machines," says Rupert. "Then I came back with him, in a flying boat . . ." "Do you like it?" asks the man cheerfully. "I made it myself, you know. In fact, I made all the clockwork toys in the castle . . ." "Even the little man?" asks Rupert. "Oh, Wolfgang?" smiles the Toymaker. "He's my finest yet. I often send him out to search for new songs . . ."

"Why do you gather songs?" asks Rupert. "For my Master's collection!" sighs the Toymaker. "Every toy I make needs a new one . . ." Removing a small wax cylinder from one of the recording devices, he shows Rupert a model bird that's ready. "All it needs is a song," he smiles and opens a little door. The moment the cylinder is placed inside, the bird starts to flap its wings and sing. "It's so lifelike!" blinks Rupert. "Yes," says the Toymaker. "I always use real songs . . ."

RUPERT HEARS ABOUT THE KING

"I made the King a dancing toy
When he was just a little boy."

"He still collects them, only now
They have to all be new somehow!"

A jangling bell begins to ring –
"An urgent summons from the King!"

"His Majesty will be upset!
My next toy isn't ready yet . . ."

"It all started long ago, when His Majesty was just a little boy," explains the Toymaker. "In those days he was thrilled with everything I made, even the simplest doll. The trouble is, the King still demands a new toy every week, each more elaborate and ambitious than the last. I do my best, but it's hard to keep coming up with something new." "All those toys!" gasps Rupert. "No wonder you have stolen so many songs. There must be hundreds in the King's collection . . ."

"I hadn't thought of it as stealing songs, admits the Toymaker. "I always . . ." Before he can say more, a nearby bell rings urgently and he jumps to his feet with a cry of alarm. "The King's summons!" he gasps. "His Majesty is expecting a new toy to be delivered, but it isn't quite finished." "What is it?" asks Rupert. "A dancing figure," says the old man. "It's nearly done, but the King won't hear of any delay. It always puts him in a terrible temper. Dear me! What am I to do?"

RUPERT SUGGESTS A TRICK

*"I know!" says Rupert. "Why don't I
Take the doll's place? It's worth a try . . ."*

*The Toymaker agrees. "This way
We'll show the King without delay."*

*"At last!" the King cries. "What have you
Brought me this time? What does it do?"*

*"A dancing bear! But where's its key?"
The King demands impatiently.*

Rupert thinks hard for a moment, then sees how he can help the Toymaker and perhaps get back the Nutwood songs . . . "I'll pretend to be the new toy!" he declares. "The King's never seen me, and the figures you make are so lifelike he'll never suspect that I'm real." "Do you think it might work?" says the old man. "I don't want to keep him waiting, but he'd be furious if he found out . . ." "Let's try!" says Rupert. The next moment the pair are hurrying off towards the King's Chamber . . .

"At last!" cries the King when he catches sight of the Toymaker . . . "Whatever have you brought me this time? It looks just like a little bear!" "Quite so, Your Majesty!" replies the old man. "But this is a very special dancing bear . . ." "Dancing?" smiles the King. "How splendid! But where do you wind it up? I can't see any key!" "That's why it's so special," says the Toymaker hurriedly. "No need for a key. No need to wind it up. Just tell it when to begin and it dances for you straightaway!"

RUPERT PRETENDS TO BE A TOY

*"This new toy is a special kind
That you will never need to wind!"*

*"Bravo!" the King cries. "It can do
Handstands and perform cartwheels too!"*

*"Of all my toys I like this best!
It's even more fun than the rest!"*

*"Guards! Take the dancing bear away
And put him in my Toy Display . . ."*

"A toy that dances all by itself?" asks the King. "Impossible!" Clapping his hands, he orders a demonstration. "Good gracious!" he exclaims as Rupert springs into action. "It does dance, and looks so lifelike too . . ." After a few moments he turns to the Toymaker and asks if Rupert can stand on his hands. "Of course!" says the old man. "Phew!" gasps Rupert as he cartwheels across the room. "I never thought that pretending to be a toy would be so tiring! I hope the King stops soon!"

"Wonderful!" laughs the King as he tells Rupert to stop. "This is one of the best toys you have ever made!" "Thank you, Your Majesty!" says the Toymaker. "A few more days in the workshop and it should be able to sing as well . . ." "No need for that!" smiles the King. "It's perfect, just as it is!" Summoning the Palace Guards, he orders them to put the new toy on display with all the others. Before Rupert can do anything, he finds himself being lifted up and carried from the hall . . .

RUPERT HAS AN IDEA

The guards take Rupert back to where
The toys are stored and leave him there.

"Oh, no!" he groans. "I'm trapped in here!"
Then Rupert has a good idea . . .

As soon as it gets dark outside
He opens all the windows wide.

Then, one by one, he winds the toys –
Which sing and dance and make a noise . . .

Still pretending to be a toy, Rupert is carried back to the King's collection and stood on an empty pedestal. As the soldiers leave, the door slams shut with a clang. "Whatever shall I do?" he wonders. "The King will be furious when he finds he's been tricked, but if I don't think of something I could be here for ages." Climbing down, he begins to explore the room. "It's a shame these toys can't talk!" he murmurs. Then he suddenly sees how they might be able to help him . . .

As soon as it grows dark, Rupert begins to throw open every window in the hall. Outside, the night is silent and nobody stirs. When the last window is open, he quickly starts to wind up all the mechanical toys, which jerk into life, one after another . . . At first, the room is filled with birdsong, then, as more machines begin to play, the noise inside grows louder and louder. "Wonderful!" laughs Rupert as it reaches a deafening crescendo. "They'll hear this all over the castle!"

RUPERT MAKES A NOISE

The King and Toymaker rush in,
Both woken by the dreadful din!

"Hello!" calls Rupert. "What a row!
I think I'll try these songbirds now . . ."

"No!" cries the King. "Each time you play
A bird, its song will get away!"

"I'll only stop if you agree
To give back Nutwood's songs to me!"

As the clockwork figures dance and scurry around the hall, the noise they make becomes a terrible din. Musicians play, birds sing and babies cry, while Rupert winds up more and more machines . . . Suddenly, the doors fly open and the King appears. "What is going on in here?" he demands. "I was sound asleep, when I heard the most hideous row." "Hello!" calls Rupert. "I thought you'd come soon. You're just in time to hear these singing birds . . ."

"Stop!" cries the King. "Don't play any more! Each time you start a machine with the windows open, its song escapes into the outside world . . ." "I know!" says Rupert. "That's where they all belong! You and your Toymaker stole every one of these songs and I intend to set them free!" "Please!" begs the King. "Let me keep my favourites. I couldn't bear to lose them all . . ." "Very well!" smiles Rupert. "But only if you promise to give back all the songs you took from Nutwood . . ."

*The King agrees. "But I thought you
Were just a clockwork figure too . . ."*

*He hears what's wrong, then smiles. "I've all
The toys I need here, in this hall!"*

*"I don't need more toys! You can take
Some time off now and have a break . . ."*

*"Goodbye!" the King says. "Wolfgang's brought
Back all the Nutwood songs he caught!"*

"Agreed!" nods the King as Rupert climbs down. Then he stops and looks perplexed. "But I thought you were only a toy!" "A small deception, Your Majesty!" admits the Toymaker. "Rupert agreed to help me when he learned that the next toy I was making wasn't finished . . ." "You tricked me, too?" cries the King. Then he shakes his head and starts to laugh. "What a fool I've been!" he declares. "To go on wanting more and more toys, when the ones I have already so marvellous!"

The King is in such a good mood that he tells the Toymaker it is time he had a holiday. "There's no need to keep on making new toys," he laughs. "From now on, I'll be perfectly happy with what I've got . . ." Keeping his promise to give back the Nutwood songs, he bids farewell to Rupert as Wolfgang carries the final recording machine back to the flying boat. "No more hoarding toys!" he smiles. "I've decided to open my collection to anyone who wants to come and see it . . ."

The flying boat takes off and then
Speeds back to Nutwood once again.

"We're nearly there now!" Rupert cries.
"That church tower's one I recognise!"

The clockwork man unloads his store
Of machines – then flies off once more.

"Tell all your chums to gather round.
The missing birdsongs have been found!"

When everything is ready, Rupert climbs into the flying boat and waits for Wolfgang to work the controls. "Goodbye!" calls the Toymaker as the ship soars over the battlements. "Thank you for all your help!" As the little boat flies steadily through the night, Rupert begins to yawn and gradually falls asleep. He wakes to find that dawn has already broken and spots some familiar-looking hills. "We're nearly there!" he cries excitedly."There's the church tower and Nutwood's houses!"

Landing on the far side of Nutwood Common, Wolfgang quickly unloads the recording machines, then bows stiffly to Rupert. Without another glance, he marches back up the ramp and prepares to take off. "Goodbye!" calls Rupert, but the little man stares blankly ahead as he steers a homeward path. Rupert sets off across the Common and hasn't gone far when he spots some birds. "I've found the missing songs!" he calls. "Tell everyone who lost their tune to come and listen straightaway . . ."

RUPERT RESTORES THE LOST SONGS

The birds are all amazed as they
Each hear their own song start to play . . .

Then, one by one, they all begin
To sing – till everyone joins in!

Bill hears the birds, then runs to learn
Of Rupert's trip and his return . . .

"There's one song left! It's Edward's mum . . ."
"Let's take it back!" suggests his chum.

Rupert sets up the recording machines as groups of birds gather round excitedly. "Listen carefully!" he says, switching on one machine after another . . . "That's me!" chirps a sparrow. "I can hear my song too!" cries an astonished crow. When all the machines have stopped, Rupert tells the birds to try singing. One by one, they warble and trill in a triumphant chorus that grows louder and louder. "Wonderful!" smiles Rupert." Everything is back to normal!"

The birds are still flying about delightedly, when Rupert suddenly spots Bill Badger. "Rupert!" he cries. "What happened? How did you get back? I heard the birds and came to see what was going on. Gosh!" he says when he hears about his chum's adventure. "You were lucky the King let you go!" "Yes," says Rupert. "And he even agreed to give back all the songs. There's just one more left to return . . . "Mrs. Trunk!" cries Bill. "Let's go and see her together . . ."

RUPERT HEARS MRS. TRUNK SING

As they reach Edward's house, the pair
Both see the doctor's car parked there.

"Let's play a trick!" smiles Rupert. He
Turns the machine on secretly . . .

The doctor tells the two chums how
His patient has recovered now . . .

"Her throat's much better! She can talk
And sing The Grand Old Duke of York!"

As Rupert and Bill get nearer to Edward's house, they see Dr. Lion's car parked outside. "He must have come to see if Mrs. Trunk's voice is any better," says Bill. "It will be soon!" laughs Rupert. "All we have to do is send back her song . . ." Quietly setting up the recording machine outside an open window, he switches it on. All at once a familiar voice begins to sing The Grand Old Duke of York. "It must have been what she was singing to Pompey!" smiles Bill . . .

No sooner has the machine stopped playing than Dr. Lion appears at the door. "Hello!" he says. "I expect you've come to visit Mrs. Trunk. I'm glad to say the patient has made a complete recovery! A few spoons of linctus and she's singing better than ever!" "That's right!" laughs Edward's mother, coming to see who's there. "I could sing all day!" "How marvellous!" says Rupert as she launches into another verse of The Grand Old Duke . . .

THE END

28

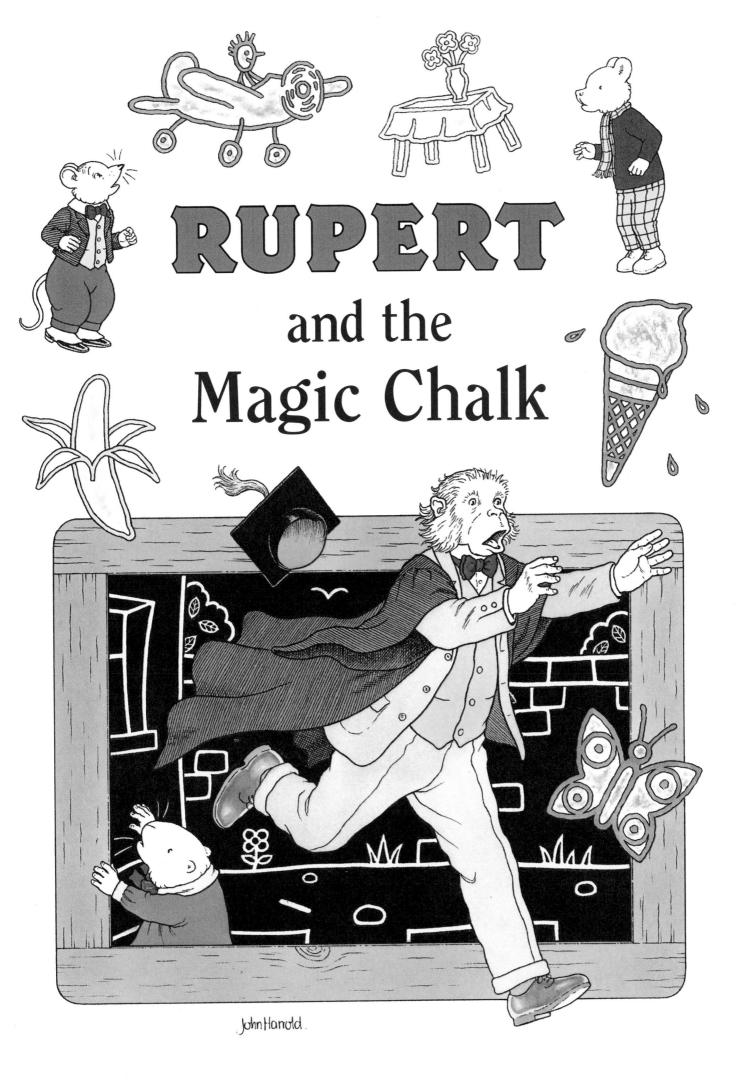

RUPERT
and the
Magic Chalk

John Harrold.

RUPERT GOES BACK TO SCHOOL

Today is the first morning when
The Nutwood chums start school again.

Their teacher says he hopes that they
Enjoyed the summer holiday.

This morning there's a treat in store –
"I'll get some chalk and you can draw . . ."

"Please pass the box round and . . . Oh, dear!
We've run out! There's none left in here!"

The summer holidays are over and it the start of a new school term for Rupert and his friends. "Hello, Bill!" calls Rupert as he hurries on his way. "Everyone is very punctual this morning! I can see Bingo, the Rabbit twins, and even Podgy's arriving on time!" The playground is full of excited chums, all catching up with each other's news. "Hello, everyone!" beams Dr. Chimp as he comes out to ring the bell. "I hope you had a good summer! It's nice to see you all again . . ."

"Welcome back to school!" says Dr. Chimp. "We'll start the new term with some drawing practice. I don't mind *what* you decide to draw, so long as you make a good job of it!" As the pals take out their slates, he rummages behind his desk and produces a large cardboard box. "Chalk!" he smiles. "You can pass it round and each take a stick . . ." As he opens the box, Dr. Chimp's smile fades. "Oh, dear!" he blinks. "It's all gone! We must have run out at the end of last term!"

RUPERT DRAWS A ROCKET

Then Tigerlily says that she
Was given some chalk recently . . .

"Bravo!" says Dr. Chimp. "Well done!
There's just enough for everyone."

"I'll draw a rocket!" Rupert cries.
"The countdown ends and up it flies!"

*"You **have** done well! I like them all*
So much we'll hang them on the wall!"

"I'm afraid we'll have to abandon our drawing lesson!" sighs Dr. Chimp. "Please, sir!" says Tigerlily. "I've got some chalk of my own. My father gave me a packet as a present. I'm sure there's enough to go round . . ." "Bravo!" cries the teacher. "We can carry on drawing after all! It's very kind of you to share your present." "That's all right!" smiles Tigerlily. "It's more fun when *everyone* does a drawing . . ." Each of the pals takes a stick of chalk and begins to draw . . .

As Rupert thinks what to draw, he suddenly has a good idea . . . "A space rocket!" he smiles. "Just like the one I saw at the cinema!" The classroom falls silent as the pals all concentrate on their drawings. "How are you getting on?" asks Dr. Chimp. "I've finished!" cries Freddie Fox. "Me too!" calls Bingo. "Come closer, so I can see what you've done!" says their teacher. "I say!" he cries. "They do look fine. Has everybody finished or are there any other drawings we haven't seen?"

RUPERT'S PAL PLAYS HOPSCOTCH

"A lovely drawing, Ottoline!
The best Triceratops I've seen . . ."

"It's break time now – then we'll talk more
About this ancient dinosaur."

Gregory tells the others, "There's
A game you make by drawing squares . . ."

"It's called hopscotch. I'll show you how
You fill in all the numbers now!"

The last drawing is by Rupert's friend Ottoline. "A dinosaur!" cries Dr. Chimp. "Look at this, everyone. Can you tell me what it's called?" "A triceratops!" calls Rupert. "That's right!" smiles his teacher. "It looks a bit fierce with those horns but they only ate leaves and plants . . ." "I still wouldn't like to meet one!" blinks Gregory. "There's not much chance of that!" laughs Dr. Chimp. "They are all extinct! Break time now," he calls. "We'll talk about dinosaurs this afternoon."

Out in the playground, Gregory tells the others that drawing with chalk has given him a good idea. "How about a game of hopscotch?" he asks. "That sounds fun!" laughs Tigerlily. "Draw out the squares and we'll all have a go . . ." Drawing on the ground with his stick of chalk, Gregory writes in the numbers to show everybody where to hop. "Nearly ready!" he calls as the chums gather round. "Who's going to have first turn?" "You!" laughs Rupert. "We'll all follow . . ."

RUPERT SEES GREGORY VANISH

The guinea-pig calls, "Hop, jump, hop!
It's easy – but you mustn't stop!"

Then, suddenly, the ground gives way –
The pals look on in shocked dismay!

A trap door snaps shut instantly,
Leaving no sign of Gregory . . .

"Fetch Dr. Chimp!" calls Rupert, then
Gasps in amazement once again . . .

Laying his chalk to one side, Gregory stands in the first square, ready to start the game. "Hop, jump, hop, jump, hop, jump!" he calls. "Your feet mustn't touch the lines and you have to keep moving . . ." Suddenly the guinea-pig's glee gives way to a cry of dismay as a trap door swings open and sends him plummeting into a gloomy pit. "What's happening?" blinks Freddy. "There wasn't a door there a moment ago!" "I know!" says Rupert and runs forward to see what's become of his chum.

To Rupert's astonishment, the mysterious door swings shut again as suddenly as it opened . . . "Gregory!" he calls. "Are you all right?" "He's shut in!" gasps Freddy. "The squares fit so snugly you can't even see a gap!" "We'll have to fetch Dr. Chimp!" says Rupert, but at that very moment, their teacher comes sprinting into the playground, running as fast as he can. "I wonder what's wrong?" blinks Bill. "It almost looks as though something is chasing him . . ."

"A dinosaur!" the teacher cries,
Unable to believe his eyes!

"They're all our drawings!" Rupert blinks.
"Each one has come to life!" he thinks.

"Oh, no!" says Tigerlily. "My
Chalk must be **magic** *– that is why!"*

The strange procession carries on,
Then Dr. Chimp spots where it's gone!

"Look out!" warns Dr. Chimp. "There's a dinosaur on the loose!" "A dinosaur?" gasps Rupert. "Why, it's Ottoline's triceratops!" "Keep back!" warns his teacher as the huge creature lumbers into the playground. "But how has my drawing come to life?" asks Ottoline. "And why has it grown so big?" Before anyone can answer, a strange procession comes following in the dinosaur's wake . . . "My rocket!" marvels Rupert. "*All* the drawings have come to life!"

As Dr. Chimp and his pupils stand gazing at the astonishing parade, Tigerlily picks up Gregory's stick of chalk and gives a cry of dismay. "It must be magic! My father always has some that he uses for conjuring tricks. The packets in his study must have got muddled up – he's given me the wrong one!" More and more chalk creations emerge from the classroom and file past Dr. Chimp. "They're escaping into Nutwood!" he gasps. "Goodness knows *what* they'll get up to there!"

RUPERT FOLLOWS A DINOSAUR

"They're bound for Nutwood High Street now,
We've got to stop them all somehow!"

"'Tis fancy dress!" old Gaffer jeers
As the bizarre parade appears.

When Growler sees the dinosaur
He says that it's breaking the law!

The creature knocks him off his feet,
Then lumbers on along the street . . .

Rupert and Dr. Chimp run out of the school gates and after the runaway drawings. "Come back!" calls the teacher but the strange procession pays no heed . . . Nutwood's inhabitants blink in amazement as the chalk creatures reach the High Street. "A fancy dress parade!" says Gaffer Jarge. "The things they get up to these days! When I was a lad, we spent all day in the classroom." "I don't think it's fancy dress," murmurs Mrs. Sheep. "The dinosaur's so heavy it's making the ground shake!"

Rupert and Bill run on ahead of the others until they reach the start of the procession. P.C. Growler has already spotted the commotion and orders the Triceratops to stop. "Halt, in the name of the Law! " he shouts, blocking the creature's path. The dinosaur pauses, then lowers its head and nudges Growler aside. "Now, then!" he warns. "Any of that and I'll place you under arrest!" The dinosaur lumbers forward and catches Growler with its tail, sending him sprawling . . .

RUPERT THINKS OF A PLAN

He isn't hurt but says the beast
Deserves to be locked up, at least!

"Come on, Bill. Perhaps you and I
Can stop them all. We've got to try!"

Then Rupert has a good idea –
"I've got some magic chalk left here!"

"We'll head them off this way!" he cries.
"I want to take them by surprise . . ."

A startled shopkeeper hurries forward to help P.C. Growler to his feet. "Are you all right?" he gasps. "Yes, thanks," murmurs the dazed policeman, "but if I ever catch that dinosaur I'll lock it up for disturbing the peace!" Before he can say any more, Rupert and Bill hurry away in pursuit of the unruly procession . . . "We've got to do something to stop them!" calls Bill. "If the Triceratops gets as far as Nutchester, it will cause havoc! The town could come to a standstill!"

As the chums chase after the runaway creatures, Rupert suddenly has a good idea. "The chalk!" he cries. "Tigerlily gave me Gregory's stick to look after when we were standing in the playground. I think I know how we can use it to sort things out . . ." Beckoning for Bill to follow, he leaves the path and sets off across the fields as fast as he can go. "We need to get far enough ahead of the procession to prepare a surprise!" he calls. "If they see what I'm up to, the plan won't work."

RUPERT DRAWS A DOOR

The two pals reach the road once more.
"That wall's the perfect place to draw!"

"Another drawing?" Bill can't see
What use the magic chalk will be . . .

"Look out!" he calls. "They're on their way.
It isn't safe for us to stay!"

But then, the door that Rupert drew
Swings open and they all march through!

Cutting across the field, Rupert joins the road again as it nears a steep bank. "Perfect!" he cries. "There will just be time to make another drawing before the chalk creatures arrive . . ." "Another drawing?" blinks Bill. "I thought we had enough already!" "This one's different!" says Rupert. He draws a long straight line as high as he can, then gets Bill to lift him on to his shoulders. "It's like drawing the goalposts for a game of football in the playground!" says Bill.

When he has finished drawing on the wall, Rupert takes the chalk and marks a pathway on the road. "Quick!" calls Bill. "The procession's nearly here." As Rupert hurries over to join him, the Triceratops lumbers along the path towards the wall. To Bill's astonishment a great door swings open, revealing a long, dark tunnel. "Magic chalk!" laughs Rupert. "*Magic* brought the creatures into Nutwood and this way it will take them out again . . ."

*"How odd!" says Dr. Chimp. "I'm sure
That tunnel wasn't here before!"*

*As Bill explains, the pals decide
To see if Gregory's inside.*

*"I'm coming with you!" Bill calls. "Wait!"
But then the door shuts. It's too late!*

*Inside the tunnel there's no light,
"It's like the middle of the night!"*

Dr. Chimp is astonished to see the chalk creatures disappearing into a secret chamber. "I didn't know there was a door here!" he blinks. "There wasn't until a few moments ago!" says Bill and explains how Rupert drew it with Tigerlily's chalk. Willie Mouse joins Rupert as the last creatures enter the tunnel. "Where are they going?" he blinks. "I'm not sure," admits Rupert. "But I'm certain it's where we'll find Gregory. All we have to do is follow the procession . . ."

Rupert and Willie follow the chalk creatures into the tunnel only to find the door swinging shut behind them . . . "Wait for me!" calls Bill, but it's too late. As the door slams shut the pair are plunged into total darkness. All they can see is the outline of a chalk boomerang, spinning through the air. "Quick!" calls Rupert. "We mustn't let it out of sight!" Hurrying forward, they find themselves back in the procession, but with no idea where the path they're following might end.

RUPERT ASKS THE WAY

The pals are left behind as they
Watch the procession speed away.

When Rupert follows it he sees
A chalk path, drawn through hills and trees . . .

"A shepherd! Let's ask if he knows
The way – and where this pathway goes!"

"Just carry on," he tells the pair.
"You'll soon reach Chalk Town – over there."

As Rupert and Willie follow the procession they find the tunnel growing wider and wider. "We've come out into a field!" blinks Rupert. The chalk creatures lumber on, then suddenly disappear over the brow of a hill . . . When Rupert and Willie follow, they are astonished to see a whole landscape of hills and trees. "*Everything* has been drawn in chalk!" cries Willie. "It's like being on a huge blackboard!" "I can see a road," says Rupert. "Let's take that and see where it leads . . ."

The two chums follow the road, which twists and turns through blackboard fields of sheep. After a while, they spot a shepherd and stop to ask directions. "Hello!" calls Rupert. "My friend and I were wondering if you can tell us where we are? We started by following a great procession but seem to have lost our way . . ." "I haven't seen any procession," says the shepherd. "But you're on the road to Chalk Town . . . Those houses mark the outskirts. Keep going and you can't miss it."

The two pals reach the town, then walk
Through streets of houses drawn with chalk . . .

"We're lost!" says Rupert. "I don't know
In which direction we should go!"

The streets seem empty, then, at last,
A boy walking his dog goes past . . .

They ask if he's seen Gregory –
"The Quarry's where he's bound to be!"

Rupert and Willie soon arrive in the middle of Chalk Town. "The houses look like drawings on a blackboard!" says Willie. "Yes!" laughs Rupert. "*Everything* here looks like a drawing. I suppose it's what you'd expect in the Land of Chalk . . ." As the pair get used to the strange surroundings, they look around for someone to ask about Gregory. "He's bound to be here somewhere!" says Willie. "I wonder?" murmurs Rupert. "So far, Chalk Town seems to be completely deserted!"

Although Chalk Town seems empty, the chums finally spot a young boy out walking his dog . . . "Hello!" calls Rupert. "We're looking for a friend of ours. I wonder if you've seen him . . ." The boy listens carefully to his description of Gregory then shakes his head. "I haven't seen anyone like that!" he says, "But he might be with the others, up at the Quarry . . ." "Quarry?" blinks Rupert. "Yes," says the boy. "Where they dig for chalk. Everyone in Chalk Town works there!"

RUPERT SEES A QUARRY

The chums set off without delay,
Then spot a sign which points the way.

"Look!" Rupert marvels. All around
Are men, digging chalk from the ground . . .

The pals explain that they have come
To try to find their missing chum.

"Try Processing! I think they had
A new recruit – an eager lad!"

Following the boy's directions, Rupert and Willie set off along the road through Chalk town and past a large sign which points to the quarry. Peering down, they are astonished to see a huge white gash in the hillside with teams of men chipping away at the rock . . . "It looks enormous!" gasps Rupert. "I wonder if Gregory is somewhere down there with them?" asks Willie. "I don't know," says Rupert. "Let's go and ask if anyone has seen him . . ."

Clambering down to the chalk face, Rupert and Willie look anxiously around for someone to ask about Gregory . . . "New recruits?" calls a man with a clipboard. "I expect you saw our advert for vacancies . . ." "Not exactly!" explains Rupert. "We were looking for a friend of ours who might have joined you earlier . . ." "From Chalk Town?" asks the man. "No," explains Rupert. "He lives with us in Nutwood . . ." "Try Processing," suggests the foreman. "That's where newcomers usually start."

RUPERT LOOKS FOR GREGORY

Inside the building the pair see
Chalk processing machinery . . .

"Hello!" calls Rupert. "Is it true
There's someone working here that's new?"

The first man sends the chums to where
The sticks of chalk are packed. "Try there . . ."

"A guinea-pig? Why, yes! I'm sure
He's working in the room next door . . ."

Inside the building, Rupert and Willie find workers from the quarry loading chalk boulders into a huge machine . . . A tremendous clanking sound fills the air as the rocks are pounded and pummelled into dust. The men are so busy that nobody notices the chums peeping round the door. "Hello!" shouts Rupert above the noise. "We've come to look for a friend of ours called Gregory . . ." "Try the Packing Department," suggests one of the men. "I think there's a new arrival working there."

Rupert and Willie walk towards the far end of the building, where the machine is pouring out hundreds of sticks of newly made chalk. As it tumbles down a chute, the chalk is packed into boxes. "Is this the Packing Department?" asks Rupert. "I've come to look for a friend of mine, called Gregory . . ." "The young guinea-pig who's just joined us!" smiles a man. "He's hard at work in the next building. Through that door and keep going. You're bound to see him straightaway . . ."

RUPERT FINDS HIS CHUM

"At last!" cries Rupert, glad they've found
Their missing schoolmate, safe and sound.

"Hello!" smiles Gregory. "What fun!
I'm sending chalk to everyone . . ."

"We can't stay in Chalk Town but how
Will we get back to Nutwood now?"

"That box says Nutwood!" Rupert blinks.
"There must be a way back . . ." he thinks.

As the door swings open, Rupert finally spots Gregory, sitting at a desk with a large pot of glue and a pile of labels. "Hello!" calls the little guinea-pig. "Isn't this fun! I've always wondered how chalk was made. First I had a guided tour of the Quarry and then they let me help in the Packing Department . . ." "What are you doing?" asks Willie. "Sticking address labels on all the boxes!" smiles Gregory. "You'd be amazed at the different places they go – all over the world!"

Rupert and Willie are glad that Gregory is safe but can't think how to go about leaving the Land of Chalk. "I was having such fun, I never thought about that!" admits Gregory. "There must be a way out," murmurs Rupert. "After all, we found a way in . . ." Looking round the factory, he suddenly stares at the pile of boxes. "Nutwood!" he cries. "Look, Gregory! One of the boxes is addressed to our village. All we have to do is find out how it's being sent!"

RUPERT LEADS THE WAY

A clerk says Dr. Chimp is due
More chalk. "He's who we send it to . . ."

"You've run out? Then I think that we
Should use Express Delivery!"

"Wait there!" he says and starts to draw
The pals a tiny little door . . .

"You'll soon be there. It isn't far!"
He smiles and holds the door ajar.

Gregory tells his chums that the Clerk in charge of orders keeps them written down in a big, heavy book. "Nutwood?" he smiles when Rupert shows him the box of chalk. "That must be for Dr. Chimp! He's one of our best customers. A regular order at the start of each term . . ." "But term has already started!" says Willie. "Dr. Chimp's run out of chalk. That's why he borrowed some from Tigerlily!" "Run out?" cries the Clerk. "We'd better send this Express Delivery! Follow me . . ."

The Clerk leads the chums along a dark corridor, which has a little door at the far end. "Dr. Chimp's orders normally go by post!" he says. "But as things are so urgent, I think you should deliver the chalk by hand . . ." Pulling the door open, he reveals a brightly lit room on the far side and invites the astonished pals to clamber through. "You won't have much further to go!" he promises. "Do send Dr. Chimp our apologies. I'll make sure his order is never late again!"

RUPERT AND HIS PALS RETURN

The three chums are astonished when
They find they're back at school again!

"The door just vanished!" Willie cries.
He shakes his head and rubs his eyes.

"You're back!" gasps Dr. Chimp. "I feared
The three of you had disappeared!"

The chums laugh as they show him how
He's got a box of new chalk now . . .

When Rupert and the others jump down, they are amazed to find themselves standing at the front of their classroom in Nutwood. "I told you it wasn't far!" laughs the Clerk. Rupert spins round towards the blackboard, but the little door has vanished as miraculously as it first appeared. "I don't believe it!" gasps Willie. "But we *did* all go to the Land of Chalk, didn't we?" says Gregory. "We certainly did!" nods Rupert. "And here's a box of chalk to prove it!"

The pals are still marvelling at their adventure when who should stride into the room but Dr. Chimp. . . "Rupert! Willie!" he gasps. "You're back! And young Gregory too. Thank goodness for that! I was sure you had all disappeared for ever!" "We went to the Land of Chalk!" cries Willie. "The Land of where?" blinks his teacher. "Chalk!" laughs Rupert. "They sent you this box by special delivery. Very special indeed . . ."

THE END

RUPERT

*The Bears have come on holiday
To spend a week at Rocky Bay.*

It is the middle of summer. Rupert and his family are on their way to Rocky Bay, together with Bill Badger, who is coming with them too. "There's the sea!" calls Rupert excitedly. "Yes!" smiles his mother. "Isn't it lovely!" When the train arrives, everyone follows Mr. Bear to their guest house. "Hello!" calls the landlady. "It's so nice to see you all again. You've brought the sunshine with you. There isn't a cloud in the sky!"

and the Whale

"Our guest house isn't very far,
It's called the Sea View – here we are!"

His Mum unpacks, but Rupert's more
Concerned to play down by the shore . . .

While his parents unpack, Rupert asks if he and Bill can go to the beach to explore. "Of course!" smiles Mrs. Bear. "But don't wander off too far . . ." The two chums decide to visit their old friend, Cap'n Binnacle. "There's his cabin on the clifftop," says Rupert. As the pair climb the path they wonder what new treasures the Captain will have to show them. "He's always adding to his collection of things from the sea!" laughs Rupert.

"Let's climb up to the Captain's shack –
It's at the top of that steep track."

When Cap'n Binnacle sees who
Is there he calls, "Ahoy, you two!"

"I've something new for you to see . . ."
"A flag!" cries Rupert, eagerly.

"I've more flags here – the sort ships fly
At sea to send their signals by . . ."

"Each flag means something! You can spell
Out words by using them as well."

"Ahoy there!" calls Cap'n Binnacle as he spots the chums. "I heard you were on your way to Rocky Bay. Good to have you back aboard!" Rupert and Bill always enjoy visiting the Captain's cabin and seeing what is new in his collection of relics from the sea. "I *have* got something to show you!" he laughs. "Actually, you can see it from down on the beach . . ." "A new flag!" cries Rupert. "It's got a ship's wheel." "Well spotted!" chuckles the Captain. "I made it myself . . ."

Cap'n Binnacle tells the chums that he has more flags for them to see inside his cabin. "These are proper signalling flags!" he declares. "A shipmate of mine sent me a full set as a reminder of our days at sea." Rupert is fascinated by the colourful display and asks why the flags are different shapes. "They all mean different things," explains his friend. "Some stand for letters and others for numbers. You can use them to spell out messages for far-off ships to read across the waves . . ."

RUPERT HEARS ABOUT THE WHALES

*"Flags aren't the only thing that's new,
I've got some other news for you . . ."*

*"A school of whales came yesterday
I saw them swimming in the bay!"*

*"Keep careful watch!" he tells the pair.
"Tomorrow they might still be there . . ."*

*The pals walk back. "I'd no idea
That whales were ever seen near here!"*

The pals are so interested in Cap'n Binnacle's flags that he promises to teach them what they all stand for. "You could send us messages!" says Bill. "Good idea!" chuckles the Captain. As they look at flags, Cap'n Binnacle tells them there is something else they should keep a look out for . . . "Whales!" he cries. "I saw a whole school of them out across the bay! They've never been so close to land. Just like the old days, when whales swam alongside our ship!"

Cap'n Binnacle tells Rupert and Bill how he watched the whales swim into Rocky Bay, then back out to deeper water. "At first I thought they must be dolphins, but they were far too big for that! Keep your eyes open, lads, and perhaps you'll see them too." "Do you think they'll still be here tomorrow?" asks Bill as the pals hurry back for tea. "I don't know," says Rupert. "Dolphins sometimes stay for ages, but whales are different. We'll just have to wait and see . . ."

RUPERT GOES TO THE BEACH

Next morning the chums hurry out
To see if whales are still about . . .

"Come on!" calls Rupert. "Follow me!
Across the rocks, down to the sea!"

"There's no sign of them!" Bill sighs. "They
Must have got bored and swum away!"

The pair play on the beach until
Rupert spots something, "Come here, Bill!"

Next morning, Rupert and Bill are up early and hurry down to the beach as soon as they have finished breakfast. "Exploring again?" says Mrs. Bear. "Be careful you don't get cut off by the tide!" When the chums reach the shore, they find the sea has gone out, leaving a wide stretch of sand with nobody else in sight. "We're the first ones here!" laughs Bill. "Come on!" calls Rupert. "I'll race you to the rocks!" Leading the way, he scrambles over the boulders towards the next bay . . .

Gazing out to sea, the chums look excitedly for any sign of whales . . . "I can't see any!" declares Bill. "Me neither!" says Rupert. "I suppose they must have gone." The pair are so pleased at having the beach to themselves, they soon forget their disappointment and start to play happily. "Watch this jump!" calls Rupert. "Easy!" laughs Bill. "My turn now . . ." After a while Rupert climbs up to peer round the next headland. "Bill!" he cries. "Come and see!"

RUPERT FINDS A STRANDED WHALE

"Look!" Rupert points, but what's he seen?
"It looks just like a submarine . . ."

The pals get nearer. Rupert blinks –
"A whale, that's what it is!" he thinks.

The chums stand dumbstruck when they reach
The whale. "It's stranded on the beach!"

The mighty creature spots the pair
And gives them both a mournful stare . . .

Bill scrambles up to see what Rupert has spotted. "Something enormous on the beach!" he blinks. "It looks like a submarine." "Or a whale!" cries Rupert. "Do you think it's real?" asks Bill. "It might be a model, like the dinosaurs at Shrimpton Sands . . ." "I wonder?" says Rupert. "Whales *do* sometimes swim in close to the shore. When the tide goes out there's always a risk of them getting stuck . . ." The chums hurry forward to take a closer look at the enormous creature lying motionless on the sand.

The astonished pals reach the huge whale. "What a find!" says Bill. "We must be the first to see it." The pair stand gazing at the enormous creature, wondering what to do next. "We can't just leave it here!" says Rupert. "It needs to get back to the sea." "It will be too heavy to move," warns Bill. "We'll have to wait for the tide to turn . . ." The whale stares sadly at the chums. "Don't worry!" says Rupert. I'm sure there's *something* we can do to help!"

RUPERT MEETS THE BEACHCOMBERS

"We'll go for help!" says Bill, but then
A call makes them turn back again . . .

"It's Tad! His whole Beachcomber crew
Has come to help the great whale too!"

"The whale can't move till High Tide comes,"
The Beachcomber tells both the chums.

"By fetching water we can try
To keep its skin from getting dry . . ."

The two pals decide to tell Cap'n Binnacle about the stranded whale. As they set off, Rupert suddenly hears somebody calling his name. Looking round, he spots a group of familiar figures, in stripy swimsuits and shell-shaped hats. "Beachcombers!" he gasps. At the head of the procession is a boy called Tad, who befriended Rupert and Bill on one of their earlier visits to Rocky Bay. "Hello!" he smiles. "You're just in time to come and help us . . ."

Tad explains that he and the other beachcombers discovered the stranded whale when they started to rake the sand at first light . . . "I've never found anything like it!" he gasps. "The largest creature in the sea!" "The poor thing can't move until the tide comes in!" says Rupert. "I know!" says Tad. "That's why we went to get buckets. If we all pour water over its skin, it won't dry out in the sunshine. You can join us, if you like. The more there are, the better it will be . . ."

RUPERT GOES FOR HELP

Each rescuer fills up a pail
Then douses down the gasping whale . . .

"Old Cap'n Binnacle might know
Another way that's not so slow!"

When Rupert's friend hears what is wrong
He soon agrees to come along.

"Bless me!" he marvels. "Run aground!
It lost its bearings, I'll be bound . . ."

Rupert and Bill help the beachcombers throw water over the stranded whale . . . "It's the only thing I can think of to protect it from the sun!" says Tad. "We'll just have to carry on until the tide comes in." "That could take ages!" says Rupert. "There must be something we can do before then . . ." He stops for a moment, then tells the others he has decided to fetch Cap'n Binnacle. "The Captain knows all about whales. He might know a way of getting it back into the water . . ."

Leaving Bill to help the beachcombers, Rupert runs back along the beach to Cap'n Binnacle's cabin. The old man is surprised to see him in such a hurry and even more surprised when he hears what is wrong. "Bless me!" he cries. "I've heard of such strandings but I can't remember ever seeing such a thing at Rocky Bay . . ." The pair set off at once and soon spot the beached whale, lying on the shore. "Run aground!" gasps the Captain. "It must have lost its bearings and strayed off course!"

RUPERT HAS AN IDEA

*"Sand sprites!" the Captain blinks. "So you
Are real! The tales I've heard are true . . ."*

*"I've seen a lot of whales before
But none were stranded on the shore!"*

*"The next High Tide here isn't due
For hours. There's nothing we can do!"*

*But Rupert thinks he knows a way
To raise the tide at Rocky Bay . . .*

When they reach the stranded whale, Cap'n Binnacle is amazed to find a group of Beachcombers keeping it cool with buckets of water. "Sand sprites!" he cries. "I've often heard tale of them but never actually seen one before . . ." "We've seen *you*!" says Tad. "Collecting shells and old driftwood down by the water's edge." "Aye!" nods the Captain. "There are lots of interesting things carried in on the tide, though I've never found anything as big as a whale . . ."

Taking a well-thumbed book from his jacket pocket, Cap'n Binnacle tells the chums that he will look up the time of the next High Tide to see how much longer the whale will be stranded. "There isn't one due for hours!" he groans. "Tad and his friends will never be able to keep it cool for that long!" Rupert thinks hard, then asks him to come back to the cabin straightaway. "No time to explain!" he says. "There are some things there we need. I've had a good idea!"

RUPERT TAKES A FLAG

*"King Neptune rules the waves: Let's show
A signal flag he'll spot below . . ."*

*"This message looks ideal to me –
I need assistance urgently!"*

*"We'll need a lead weight and some rope.
This coil should be enough, I hope!"*

*The pair climb down some steps to reach
A dingy, moored down by the beach.*

On the way to the cabin, Rupert explains that it is the Captain's new flags he wants. "We can use them to send a message," he declares. "A message?" blinks Cap'n Binnacle. "Whoever to?" "King Neptune!" says Rupert. "He rules the waves, so I thought we'd ask him to send an early tide . . ." "Good idea!" nods the Captain. "This flag with the red cross should do the trick. It means you require immediate assistance. As soon as Neptune spots it he's bound to come and see what's wrong . . ."

As well as the signalling flag, Rupert and his friend take a rope and a heavy weight. "No point in running it *up* the mast!" says the Captain, "It will have to be *under* the water for Neptune to see . . ." The chums hurry back down to the shore, where Cap'n Binnacle's rowing boat lies moored. "She's a long way from the sea!" he warns. "Don't worry!" says Rupert. "We can both pull together." "Right you are!" cries the Captain. "Emergency launching. Full speed ahead!"

RUPERT SENDS A MESSAGE

They drag the boat down to the sea,
Then start to row out hurriedly.

"That marker buoy's the place to try.
King Neptune's H.Q.'s quite close by . . ."

The Captain stops and ships his oars.
"It's time to try this plan of yours!"

Rupert pays out the rope. "I'm sure
Our flag has reached the ocean floor."

Rupert and Cap'n Binnacle drag the dinghy to the water's edge, then jump aboard as it starts to float clear. "Well done!" calls the Captain. "I'll row out to sea until you tell me to stop . . ." The pair make steady progress across the bay, searching for the best place to send their message. "Aim for that marker buoy!" calls Rupert excitedly. "It's where Bill and I first met the Merboy. King Neptune's Headquarters can't be far below." "Aye, aye, Rupert!" calls Cap'n Binnacle.

Cap'n Binnacle rows forward slowly, then stops as they reach the marker buoy. "Thread the flag on to the rope!" he calls to Rupert. "We'll fit this weight as well, to make sure it reaches the bottom . . ." When everything is ready, Rupert throws the heavy weight overboard and starts to pay out the rope. "We require immediate assistance!" he says. "I hope King Neptune spots our message! I don't suppose anyone has ever used flags to signal underwater before . . ."

RUPERT TELLS THE MERBOY

The Merboy comes to ask what's wrong,
"I saw this as I swam along!"

"A whale's been beached at Rocky Bay!
We need a High Tide straightaway . . ."

"To turn the tide's a tricky task!
I'll show you who you ought to ask."

"This way!" he calls and swims off to
An island that comes into view.

At first Rupert's message seems to have gone unnoticed but then a youthful figure pops up, clutching the flag. "The Merboy!" cries Rupert. "Bless me!" gasps Cap'n Binnacle. "A lad with a fish's tail!" "I saw your message!" says the Merboy. "We learnt ships' flags at school. What's the matter?" he demands. "Have you sprung a leak or lost an oar?" "It's not us!" explains Rupert. "A whale has been stranded on the beach and I want King Neptune to send an early tide . . ."

To Rupert's dismay, the Merboy explains that King Neptune is away on a trip to the South Seas. "We'll have to ask the Tide Master to help!" he declares. "I'll lead the way, while you both follow in your boat." As Rupert wonders where they are going, Cap'n Binnacle gives a sudden cry. "Land ahoy! We're heading towards an island . . ." "Neptune's Isle!" calls their guide. "It's too small to show up on maps and so rocky that most folk never give it a second glance."

57

RUPERT ENTERS NEPTUNE'S CAVE

"A secret cave!" the Captain calls.
"Where smugglers used to hide their hauls!"

"You're nearly right!" the Merboy cries.
"It's where King Neptune's H.Q. lies!"

The Merboy says that he will swim
Ahead while Rupert follows him.

"The Tide Master!" blinks Rupert. "He
Must be who we have come to see!"

When they reach the island, Rupert spots a mysterious cave by the water's edge. "Looks like a smugglers' hideaway!" says Cap'n Binnacle. "It's well hidden!" laughs the Merboy "But Neptune's Cave has more valuable treasures than pirate gold – it's a secret entrance to our undersea headquarters!" Cap'n Binnacle rows alongside a rocky ledge, then steadies the boat as Rupert climbs out. "This way, Rupert!" calls the Merboy. "The path leads right into the cave . . ."

Rupert follows the Merboy into the water-filled cave. Inside he finds a large cavern supported by slender columns of rock. At the back of the cave is a curtain of seaweed, which the Merboy draws aside to reveal the Tide Master's office. "Who's there?" blinks a startled turtle. "We don't allow sightseeing tours, you know. Can't spare the time to show folk round!" "I'm sorry to bother you," says the Merboy. "But Rupert and I have come to ask your help . . ."

RUPERT ASKS FOR AN EARLY TIDE

*"I've come to ask if you can send
An early tide to help my friend . . ."*

*"I'm sorry! That would never do.
I can't send tides until they're due!"*

*"Please help us save the whale! I'm sure
The Beachcombers can't do much more . . ."*

*The turtle blinks. "A whale, you say?
All right! High Tide is on its way!"*

Rupert and the Merboy tell the Tide Master how a whale has been stranded on the beach at Rocky Bay. "It needs an early tide to get back to the sea!" says Rupert. "An early tide?" gasps the turtle. "Yes," says the Merboy. "High Tide isn't due for ages yet . . ." "That's right!" snaps the turtle. "Which is when it will arrive! I can't send tides early just because someone asks me! There's an official time-table to keep to! King Neptune's the only one who can send *special* tides."

"*Please* help us!" begs Rupert. "I don't think the Beachcombers can save the whale by themselves . . ." "Beachcombers?" blinks the turtle. "What have *they* got to do with all this?" When he hears how Tad and his friends have been keeping the whale cool by fetching buckets of water, the turtle looks thoughtful, then turns to the Rocky Bay lever. "I suppose it won't do much harm!" he shrugs. "Highly irregular, but it *is* to help a creature of the deep. Off you go now – High Tide's on its way!"

RUPERT HURRIES BACK

*"High tide's due soon! We'd better go
And let Tad and the others know!"*

*"Good luck!" the Merboy calls. "I'll tell
The sea creatures it's due as well . . ."*

*The friends run back along the shore,
Towards the stranded whale once more.*

*"As High Tide won't arrive just yet,
There's one more thing that we can get . . ."*

Rupert and the Merboy hurry to tell Cap'n Binnacle how the Tide Master has agreed to send a special tide. "We've got to let Tad know!" says Rupert. "He'll need to be ready the moment the sea starts to rise . . ." Cap'n Binnacle agrees to row back to Rocky Bay as quickly as he can. "I'd better let the undersea dwellers know what to expect!" says the Merboy. "A freak tide could cause trouble for sea creatures who weren't expecting it. I'll dive down and spread the word before it's too late!"

When they arrive at Rocky Bay, Rupert and Cap'n Binnacle find Bill and the Beachcombers still hard at work, fetching buckets of water. "Good news!" calls Rupert. "A special tide is on the way! We shouldn't have much longer to wait." "I hope it does the trick!" says Tad. "The whale's so heavy it might not float away." "I've been wondering about that too," says Rupert. "I think I know what we need to do, but first of all we'll have to pay a visit to Beachcomber Castle . . ."

RUPERT BORROWS SOME FLOATS

The moment Tad hears what they need
He hurries off at breakneck speed.

The pals call at Lost Property.
"We need your help! Emergency!"

Tad asks to borrow water-wings
Beachballs, air-beds and rubber rings . . .

The pair rush back along the beach.
"Quick!" Rupert calls. "All take one each!"

Rupert and Tad hurry along the beach to a hidden cove where the Beachcombers' castle lies. Ignoring the great fort, Rupert runs to a nearby kiosk, which carries a sign reading, "Lost Property". "I need to borrow some things from your store!" he explains to Tad. "I think they'll help the whale to float, if we can manage to gather enough. "Hello!" blinks the lobster in charge. "How can I help you? Is it something you've lost or have you come to report an unusual find?"

To the lobster's amazement, Rupert explains that he wants to borrow the Beachcombers' entire store of beachballs and inflatable mattresses . . . "To save the stranded whale!" he adds. "They're to help him float in the shallow water . . ." "First it's buckets, now you want balls as well!" tuts the lobster. "Very well! But make sure you bring them back." Rupert and Tad wheel their load across the sand to the others. "Quick, everyone!" calls Rupert. "Come and help blow up these floats!"

RUPERT'S CHUMS HELP THE WHALE

"There isn't much time left!" he cries.
"The water has begun to rise . . ."

"We'll pack these round to help him float,
Then try to launch him, like a boat!"

The rising tide reaches the whale –
Waves start to lap around his tail . . .

"It's working!" Bill calls happily.
The whale drifts slowly out to sea.

The scene on the beach is one of frantic activity as everyone blows up beachballs and floats from the lobster's store . . . "We'll have to be quick to catch the tide!" warns Rupert. "The sea has already started to rise." Following Rupert's lead, the Beachcombers pack rubber rings and beachballs all around the stranded whale. "You won't need to wait much longer now," Rupert whispers. "As soon as you're afloat again, we'll try to push you out to deeper water."

By the time the chums have finished, gentle waves are lapping round the whale's tail. "Get into position!" Tad calls to his fellow Beachcombers. "Now wait until I gave the word . . ." Rupert and Bill look on anxiously as the tide advances up the beach. "He's afloat!" calls Cap'n Binnacle. "Time to cast off and put out to sea . . ." "Heave!" cries Tad. "Keep pushing away from the shore." "It's working!" laughs Bill. "One more shove and the whale will reach deep water!"

RUPERT SEES THE WHALE IS SAFE

The whale dives down and disappears –
"It's swimming!" everybody cheers . . .

They're even more delighted when
It suddenly bobs up again!

More whales appear off Rocky Bay.
"A whole school must be on the way!"

The Merboy's with them. "They've all come
To welcome back their stranded chum!"

Slowly but surely, the Beachcombers guide the whale out to sea. At first it drifts motionless on the floats, then suddenly dives down with a flick of its mighty tail. "Hurray!" cheers Rupert as the whale bobs up again, squirting a jet of water through its blowhole. "Bravo!" cries Tad. "It's safe and sound . . ." "Fit as a fiddle!" nods Cap'n Binnacle as the whale blows another spout high in the air. "You youngsters did well to get it back into the water!"

As the chums talk, Rupert suddenly spots more whales, further out to sea. "It's a whole school!" marvels Cap'n Binnacle. "I can see the Merboy!" laughs Rupert. "They're giving him a ride!" The newcomers gather in a circle round the whale that has been rescued. "They're his brothers and sisters!" explains the Merboy. "The whole family were swimming past Rocky Bay when he suddenly disappeared!" The delighted whales beam happily as they hear all about their brother's adventure . . .

The whales swim off as everyone
Agrees the rescue bid was fun . . .

"Goodbye!" calls Tad. "Enjoy your stay
And the rest of your holiday!"

"Ahoy there, Mrs. Bear! You see
I've got two shipmates here with me!"

"Just wait until you hear their tale
Of how we saved a stranded whale!"

Reunited with his family, the rescued whale blows a final jet of water then sets out towards the open sea. "Fare thee well!" calls Cap'n Binnacle. "We'll not forget you in Rocky Bay!" "I expect the whale will remember us too!" laughs Bill. "I'm glad we were able to help him!" says Tad. "Me too!" nods the Merboy. "Thanks to Rupert's plan!" "It's time for us to go now," announces Tad. "Enjoy the rest of your holiday!" "Thanks!" calls Rupert and waves goodbye to the Beachcombers.

As the chums reach the main beach, they spot Rupert's parents. "Hello!" calls Mrs. Bear. "We've found you at last." "We've been with Cap'n Binnacle," says Bill. "Learning more about the sea?" asks Rupert's father. "Aye!" chuckles the Captain. "Only this time it's me who's done the learning. Beachcombers, Merboys and a great whale stranded on the shore. If I hadn't seen 'em with my own eyes I'd never have believed it!"

THE END

RUPERT
and the
Water Boatman

John Harrold

RUPERT HEARS A TALL STORY

A football match is underway . . .
"Let's ask the Fox brothers to play!"

But Ferdy says they're off to take
A swim in Nutwood's nice warm lake . . .

"The weather's too cold! They'll both freeze!"
Laughs Podgy. "I think it's a tease!"

The others say they think the same
And happily resume the game.

It is a chilly autumn day. Rupert and his pals are playing football together on Nutwood Common. "We could really do with a few more players!" puffs Podgy. "There are the Fox brothers," cries Rupert. "I wonder if they would like to join us?" "No, thanks," says Ferdy when Rupert calls him over. "Normally we'd love to play, but today we're off for a swim." "A swim?" gasps Rupert. "Where?" "In the lake!" says Freddy. "It's ever so warm. We're just on our way there now . . ."

"Swimming in the lake!" laughs Podgy. "It must be some sort of joke. The water will be freezing at this time of year!" "It does seem a bit unlikely," admits Rupert. "But if the Foxes aren't really going swimming, I wonder what they are up to?" "Who knows?" shrugs Algy. "They're always playing jokes of some kind . . ." He kicks the ball high into the air and soon the chums have forgotten all about the mystery as the game carries on, with Rupert scoring the first goal.

RUPERT IS SURPRISED

Rupert is on his way home when
He sees the Fox brothers again.

They rub their fur as they walk by,
"We've got to rush home to get dry!"

Next morning Rupert's keen to see
If he can solve the mystery . . .

He nears the lake. "There's Podgy too!
Wait!" Rupert calls. "I'll come with you."

When the chums finish playing football, it is time for Rupert to go home for tea. As he hurries across the Common he spots the Foxes, coming back from the direction of the lake. To his astonishment they are both rubbing themselves dry with their towels. "So you *did* go swimming after all!" he gasps. "Of course!" smiles Freddy. "The water was lovely and warm, even better than last time . . ." "Can't stop!" cries his brother. "We've got to get indoors before we catch a chill in this cold air."

Next morning, Rupert is still puzzled by the Foxes' strange behaviour and decides to visit the lake. He hasn't gone far when he meets Podgy, heading across the Common in the same direction. "I'm sure they're playing a trick on us!" his friend declares. "The only way to call their bluff is to find out what the lake really feels like. It's always fairly chilly, even in the summer . . ." "We'll soon find out!" says Rupert. "It's not far away, just behind those tall trees."

RUPERT FEELS THE WATER

The two chums reach the lake, which seems
So hot now that the water steams!

"A fountain!" Podgy cries. "I say!
That wasn't here the other day."

They feel the water. "Goodness me!
*It **is** hot. How extraordinary!"*

Then Rupert notices the ground –
"Podgy! Look at these tracks I've found!"

Curious to see if the Foxes can really have gone for a swim, Rupert and Podgy hurry through the trees until they reach the edge of the lake. "I don't believe it!" gasps Rupert. "The water's steaming!" "Amazing!" blinks Podgy. "No wonder they didn't feel cold!" As the two pals stand staring at the lake, Podgy suddenly notices something even more peculiar. "There's a fountain!" he cries. "It's bubbling up out of the water!" "How odd!" says Rupert. "Let's take a closer look."

Running down to the water's edge, the two pals roll up their sleeves to feel for themselves how hot it is. "Extraordinary!" cries Rupert as he trails a hand in the water. "It's just like a warm bath!" "Perhaps we should *all* go swimming!" laughs Podgy. "The lake seems hotter now than it did in the summer." "There's definitely something very odd going on," murmurs Rupert as he climbs to his feet. Then he gives a cry of surprise. "Podgy! Come and look at these strange footprints . . ."

RUPERT'S PAL FINDS A BOAT

*"Come on!" he says. "Let's try to find
Whoever left this trail behind . . ."*

*The tracks start by the lakeside where
A pole sticks up – "There's something there!"*

*"A boat!" says Podgy. "Someone's stored
All sorts of little jars aboard!"*

*"I wonder what's inside them?" he
Says."I'll just take a look and see . . ."*

"Gosh!" cries Podgy, looking at the footprints. "I wonder who made them?" "I don't know," says Rupert. "Perhaps it wasn't a *person* at all . . ." Although they both feel rather nervous, the chums can't resist trying to find out where the footprint trail leads – and slowly start to follow them along the lakeside path. All of a sudden, Rupert stops and points to a strange sight. "There's something down by the water's edge," he whispers. "Yes," says Podgy, "but what can it be?"

"A boat!" marvels Podgy. "Someone must have moored it here while they went for a walk round the lake." "What a strange shape!" says Rupert. "It doesn't look like an ordinary rowing boat. For one thing, there aren't any oars . . ." "Look inside," says Podgy. "It's full of all sorts of bottles and jars!" "Don't touch any of them," warns Rupert, but Podgy doesn't seem to hear. "I only want to find out what's inside," he says. "You keep watch, in case the owner comes back . . ."

RUPERT'S PAL IS CAST ADRIFT

*"They're all the same! But who would take
Jars of pond-water from the lake?"*

*Then Podgy slips. "Oh, no!" he cries.
"I think I'm going to capsize!"*

*As Rupert looks on in dismay
The boat begins to drift away.*

*"Help!" Podgy calls. "What shall I do?"
"Don't worry! I'll keep up with you . . ."*

Stepping into the little boat, Podgy bends down and picks up one of the jars. "It's full of water!" he cries. "It looks as if it has come from the lake," says Rupert. "But who would want to collect bottles full of pond water?" "They're all the same!" says Podgy. "I wonder what they're for?" "You'd better put them back before anyone sees," says Rupert. Podgy agrees, but as he leans forward the boat starts to sway from side to side. "Help!" he cries. "I've lost my balance!"

As Podgy topples backwards, he grabs wildly at an upright pole, then lands in a heap at the bottom of the boat. "Oh, no!" gasps Rupert. "It's drifting free!" Before he can do anything, the boat swings away from its mooring and begins to glide out across the lake. "What shall I do?" wails Podgy. "There aren't any oars to row back!" "Don't worry!" calls Rupert. "I'll follow you along the path. As soon as you run aground, we'll be able to pull the boat ashore."

RUPERT SEES PODGY DISAPPEAR

*The boat begins to gain speed now –
"It's going by itself somehow!"*

*Then, suddenly, it swings around
And seems about to run aground.*

*Poor Podgy's sure he'll hit the rock
But then he gets another shock . . .*

*"A cave!" gasps Rupert. "He's all right!
Then Podgy's boat drifts out of sight.*

To Rupert's surprise, the little boat seems to gather speed as it drifts out across the lake. "It's moving by itself!" cries Podgy. "Impossible!" says Rupert, but as he runs along the bank the boat goes faster and faster, until he can't keep up with it any longer . . . "Perhaps it's being blown by the wind?" he thinks. The next moment, Rupert blinks in disbelief as the boat veers off towards a rocky outcrop. "Help!" calls Podgy. "If it doesn't slow down, I'm going to crash!"

As the mysterious boat speeds through the water it shows no sign of slowing down, but keeps on a steady path towards the rocky outcrop. "There's nothing I can do!" wails Podgy, bracing himself for the collision. Suddenly, he looks up and gives a gasp of surprise. "What's happened?" calls Rupert anxiously. "There's some sort of hidden cave!" cries Podgy. "It's covered with trailing plants . . ." As he speaks, the boat glides silently between two rocks and disappears from sight . . .

71

RUPERT TRIPS OVER

"I wonder where the boat has gone?"
Thinks Rupert as he hurries on.

Then Rupert trips. Next thing he feels
Himself falling head over heels!

He clambers up, amazed to see
A stranger watching anxiously . . .

"Oh dear! My jars were in your way.
I've been collecting them all day!"

"A secret cave!" gasps Rupert. "Podgy's boat must have been carried inside by an underground stream . . ." Calling out to his chum, he runs along the path by the side of the lake as fast as he can. "I wonder if Podgy can hear me?" he thinks. "I hope he hasn't gone very far . . ." Rupert is so anxious to reach the cave that he doesn't notice a small object lying on the path. His foot hits something hard as he races along and the next moment he finds himself tumbling head over heels.

Luckily, Rupert isn't hurt by the fall. He looks up in surprise as a stranger dressed in oilskins suddenly appears. "Man overboard!" he calls. "All my fault. Didn't mean to capsize you by blocking the way with my things . . ." Helping Rupert up, he points to a small wicker basket lying on the grass. "It's full of jars and bottles!" cries Rupert. "Then it must be *your* boat we saw, moored by the shore." "That's right!" smiles the man. "I left her there while I came to get more samples."

RUPERT ASKS ABOUT PODGY

*"My friend climbed in your boat but then
It disappeared from sight again!"*

*"Please tell me how to bring him back!
Is there a path or special track?"*

*"The Waterworks is where your friend
Will come to at his journey's end."*

*"That's where I work. My job's to make
Reports on problems, like this lake . . ."*

"Oh dear!" sighs Rupert and tells the man how he and Podgy couldn't resist taking a closer look at the little boat. "My friend was cast adrift, then vanished into a hidden cave!" he explains. "Not to worry!" smiles the man. "My boat will have taken itself back to the Waterworks. They all do that unless there's someone to steer." "The Waterworks?" asks Rupert as the man starts to gather his jars. "I don't understand. Who are you, and why are you collecting so many jars of water?"

"I'm a Boatman from the Waterworks!" explains the stranger. "It's our job to look after all the ponds and rivers . . . I was on my way to Nutwood to investigate a complaint from the Autumn Elves, when I suddenly noticed how hot the lake was and stopped to take some samples." "It's never been like this before," says Rupert. "No," says the Boatman. "The water's hotter now than it should be in the middle of summer. Something very odd must have happened. I don't understand it at all!"

RUPERT FOLLOWS THE ELVES

Just then, two Autumn Elves appear –
"Hello! Thank goodness that you're here!"

"This way!" an Elf calls. "Follow me,
There's a door in this hollow tree . . ."

The pair are being taken to
The Autumn Elves' secret H.Q.

"It isn't far now – through that door,
The Baths are what we called you for . . ."

As Rupert and the Boatman gaze at the lake, a shrill voice calls out, "There you are! Our Chief was beginning to think you weren't coming . . ." "Autumn Elves!" gasps Rupert. "Sorry to keep you waiting," says the Boatman. "We'd better set off straightaway." "Can I come too?" asks Rupert. "Of course," says his new friend. "I'll take you to see the Waterworks too." "This way!" calls the second Elf. His companion hurries to a nearby tree and pulls open a hidden door . . .

Inside the tree is a steep flight of steps which leads down to a rocky tunnel. "This must be the way to the Elves' Headquarters!" whispers Rupert. "Follow me, please!" the first Elf calls to the Boatman. "The Chief should be waiting for us in the Bathhouse. He told me to take you there as soon as you arrived." "I wonder what's wrong?" thinks Rupert. "Whatever can the Boatman have to do with the Chief's bath? I thought he said he was in charge of ponds and rivers . . ."

RUPERT HEARS WHAT IS WRONG

"Baths?" Rupert thinks. "It's a mistake.
I thought they'd noticed Nutwood's lake!"

"The bathwater from our supply
Is freezing cold! Please find out why!"

"It should be warm the whole year round,
Piped from a hot spring underground."

"I'll send you home a special way
So you can start without delay . . ."

Following the Elf through a door marked "Baths", Rupert and the Boatman find themselves face to face with the Chief Elf. "Thank goodness you've come to help us!" he cries. "I will if I can," says the little man, "but what's wrong? Why have you sent for me?" "Our water!" replies the Chief. "It's normally nice and warm, direct from an underground spring, but yesterday it suddenly turned icy cold. Feel for yourself! The baths are so chilly that we've had to stop using them!"

"Good gracious!" cries the Boatman. "You're quite right, the water feels freezing! I can't think what's happened – it's piped here straight from the spring!" "What can you do?" asks Rupert. "Nothing till I know what's wrong!" declares the Boatman. "I'll have to go back to Headquarters and ask for help. Somebody there might know all about it . . ." "But that could take ages!" sighs the Chief Elf. "I know! There's a shortcut. You can travel back to the Waterworks by railcar . . ."

RUPERT RIDES IN A RAILCAR

"Our railway has a special track –
A railcar will soon take you back."

The pair climb in and find that they
Are quickly speeding on their way.

The car goes fast, then faster still,
It twists and turns its way downhill . . ."

Then, at the far end of the line,
Rupert spots a "Waterworks" sign.

Rupert knows that the Autumn Elves have a special railway, with little cars that run along underground tracks. "There's a branch line that will take you all the way to the Waterworks!" the Chief declares. "All you have to do is keep the lever pressed forward until you want to stop . . ." Rupert and the Boatman climb into the railway car and are soon ready to start. "Good luck!" calls the Elf as Rupert pushes on the lever. "I hope you'll soon be able to find out what's gone wrong."

At first, the Elves' railcar glides along quite gently, then it veers off down a narrow turning and suddenly gathers speed. "Hold on tight!" calls the Boatman. "It's like a roller-coaster!" gasps Rupert. "Yes!" laughs his companion. "Our H.Q. is deep underground . . ." Eventually the car begins to slow. "We must be nearly there," says the Boatman. Sure enough, Rupert spots the end of the line and a sign reading, "Waterworks". "This way," says the Boatman. "Follow me!"

RUPERT SEES THE WATERWORKS

"This way!" the Boatman calls. They take
A pathway to a hidden lake . . .

"The Waterworks!" his guide declares
As Rupert stands amazed and stares.

The Boatman says, "You'll need a pair
Of our special pond-skates to wear . . ."

"They're what all Water Boatmen use –
Just slip them on over your shoes!"

Carefully closing the door behind him, the Boatman leads Rupert along a rocky tunnel until they reach an enormous underground lake. "There!" he says proudly, pointing to the far side. "That's the Waterworks you can see, straight ahead . . . Lots of streams and rivers start from here, so it's the perfect spot to keep an eye on them all." "But how are we going to get across the lake?" asks Rupert. "There aren't any bridges and there don't seem to be any boats!"

"Crossing a lake is easy!" laughs the Boatman. "All you need is a pair of skates . . ." "Skates?" asks Rupert. "But it's not frozen. There isn't any ice!" "Pond-skates!" declares the Boatman, reaching into his basket. "You blow them up like water-wings, then wear them on your feet." "Wonderful!" cries Rupert. "But how am *I* going to get across?" "The same way!" smiles the Boatman. "I always carry a spare set in case of emergencies. You put these on while I blow up the others . . ."

Rupert and the Water Boatman

RUPERT USES POND-SKATES

"Now we can both cross easily.
I'll lead the way, just follow me!"

"What fun!" laughs Rupert as they stride
Across the pond to the far side.

Two guards come out to meet the pair
And ask the Boatman who is there . . .

"A land-dweller! He's come ashore
To find someone he's looking for."

As soon as they are both ready, the Water Boatman steps out from the shore on to the surface of the lake. "Don't worry!" he calls to Rupert. "As long as you're wearing pond-skates it's easy to walk across to the other side . . ." Rupert steps out cautiously and begins to follow his friend. "You're right!" he laughs. "It's like walking on a giant sheet of glass!" "Not much further now," says the Boatman. "As soon as we reach the Waterworks, I'll take you inside."

No sooner have Rupert and the Water Boatman stepped ashore, than two guards come hurrying towards them. "Who's this?" they ask. "A land-dweller," says the Boatman. "He's searching for a missing friend . . ." "That must be the stranger who arrived earlier!" says the guard. "He told us some yarn about Nutwood lake being warm!" "It's true!" exclaims the Boatman. "And there's a new fountain, right in the middle! Come with me," he tells Rupert. "I'll take you to see your friend."

78

"Your friend's quite safe! Let's go and tell
The Inspector we're here as well . . ."

IT CAN'T BE HIM

GO TO PAGE 108

"Thank goodness you've come!" Podgy cries.
"They're all convinced I'm telling lies!"

"You say the lake's hot? Then it's true!
But why? And what are we to do?"

The Elves have **cold** bathwater now!
Their hot spring's warmed the lake somehow . . .

Inside the Waterworks, a maze of tunnels leads to a door marked "Head Office". "This is where we'll find your friend," the Boatman tells Rupert. He's been taken to see the Inspector . . ." Pushing it open, he announces their arrival. "*Another* land-dweller?" gasps the Inspector. "Yes," says the Boatman. "He has come from Nutwood, with important news!" "Rupert!" cries Podgy. "Thank goodness you're here! Nobody believes the lake is hot – they all think I'm making it up!"

When the Inspector hears Rupert's story, he admits that Podgy must be telling the truth . . . "I still don't understand," he complains. "*Why* has the lake grown so warm? I'ts never happened before!" Rupert suddenly thinks he knows the answer . . . "Of course!" he cries. "The lake's not the only thing that's changed temperature. While it's got warm, the Elves' baths have turned freezing cold!" "That's right!" says the Boatman. "Their hot water must be escaping into the lake!"

*"A broken pipe! We'll send a team
To mend it in a submarine . . ."*

*"Wait!" calls the Boatman. "Extra crew!
My friends and I are going too."*

*The Boatman says they'll take the same
Way to Nutwood that Podgy came.*

*"We're back on Nutwood's lake once more,
But where's the leak we're looking for?"*

"If the Elves' hot water is escaping, there must be a broken pipe!" declares the Inspector. "I'll summon a repair team straightaway . . ." "Come on!" says the Boatman. "If we hurry we should be in time to join in. You two discovered what was wrong, so it's only fair you should see what happens next!" Following him back to the lake, the pals spot a strange boat, with a diver perched on the back, "A submarine!" gasps Rupert. "Extra crew members!" the Boatman calls. "They're coming with us!"

As soon as Rupert and Podgy are safely aboard, the Boatman pulls down a glass cover and switches on the engine. "Very useful for underwater repairs!" he chuckles. "A submarine like this can go anywhere . . ." Making their way through the rocky cavern, they eventually reach a narrow opening, which leads to Nutwood lake. "As soon as we've mended the pipe, everything should go back to normal," explains the Boatman. "The only problem now is to find out where it's broken . . ."

RUPERT GOES UNDERWATER

"The fountain!" Rupert cries. "You see?
That's where the broken pipe must be!"

The submarine dives down to take
A closer look beneath the lake . . .

The pondweed sways before their eyes –
"We've found it!" everybody cries.

The diver says that he can make
A new join that will mend the break.

"The fountain!" cries Rupert. "Perhaps that's where the pipe's broken? It wasn't here before the lake grew hot . . ." "Good idea!" says the Boatman. "We'll try there first." Signalling to the diver, he presses a button on the control panel which sends the submarine plunging below the surface of the lake. "Gosh!" says Rupert. "It looks so different down here . . ." "Yes," smiles the Boatman. "Land-dwellers are always surprised! If you spot anything odd, we'll take a closer look . . ."

Before long, Rupert notices some strands of pondweed swaying from side to side. "It's the start of the fountain!" he cries. "And look, there's the broken pipe!" "Well done!" says the Boatman. "we'll drop anchor here, while the diver gets to work . . ." Climbing down from his seat, the little diver studies the pipe carefully. Opening his tool box, he takes out a spanner and fits the two pieces together. "Bravo!" cheers the Boatman. "Everything will soon be back to normal."

81

RUPERT SAYS GOODBYE

"All done!" he signals. "Good as new!
Now I'll ride back again, with you . . ."

The submarine starts up once more
And heads towards the Nutwood shore.

"Goodbye! Thank you for all you've done!"
The pals both say that it was fun.

"The Foxes won't believe it when
They come to have a swim again!"

When he has finished, the diver turns to the pals and signals that he is ready to go. "Excellent!" says the Boatman. "We'll cast off as soon as he's back on board." The submarine's engine gives a gentle hum and they rise slowly to the surface of the lake. "It will still feel warm for a while," says the Boatman. "But by this time tomorrow, the whole lake should be back to its proper temperature. The Elves' baths should be back to normal too!" he chuckles. "By now they'll be piping hot!!"

"Thanks for all your help!" says the Water Boatman as the two pals step ashore. "We would never have been able to solve the mystery without you." "It was nothing really," says Rupert. "But I did enjoy seeing the Waterworks . . ." "I say!" chuckles Podgy. "Do you think Freddy and Ferdy will try swimming in the lake again tomorrow?" "I wonder?" smiles Rupert. "They'll certainly get a surprise if they jump in without testing the water first!"

THE END

How carefully can you colour these two pictures?

Where is Gregory?

Gregory Guineapig has disappeared. Look carefully at the hopscotch squares to see where he has gone. *Answer on page 109.*

Odd One Out

Look carefully at these drawings of Tigerlily, Podgy and the Chief Elf. Sort them into pairs and put a circle around the odd ones out.

These two pictures look identical, but there are ten differences between them.
Can you spot them all? *Answers on page 109.*

Rupert's Crossword Puzzle

See if you can complete this crossword. All the answers can be found in stories from this year's annual . . .

ACROSS:

4. The person in charge of Nutwood's waterworks (9)
5. Rupert's gift to Santa (5)
7. Edward Trunk's baby brother (6)
9. Pond ------, Inflatable footware (6)
10. Where 8 down is dug from the ground (6)
12. Badger, Rupert's pal (4)
13. Tad's friends. They live in a sandcastle (12)
16. A prickly woodland creature (8)
17. Delivered by Santa Claus (8)
18. They pull Santa's sleigh (8)
25. Village where Rupert lives (7)
26. The Chinese conjurer's daughter (9)
27. Dr. ----, Nutwood's physician (4)

DOWN:

1. Another word for Looking-glass (6)
2. Rupert's greedy chum (5)
3. Retired sea-captain from Rocky Bay (8)
6. The name of Rupert's prickly woodland chum, see 15 across (6)
8. Used to write on blackboards (5)
11. A large sea creature, sometimes left stranded (5)
12. The old Professor's servant (6)
13. Where 19 down get washed (5)
14. Stolen by a royal toymaker (5)
15. Knowledgeable bird (4, 3, 3)
17. Lost --------, collected by 13 across (8)
19. They tend Nutwood's plants and trees in 22 down (5)
20. Freddy and Ferdy Fox get into this! (3, 5)
21. A creature who controls the tides (6)
22. The season that follows Summer (6)
23. Sung at Christmas (6)
24. Dr -----, Rupert's teacher (5)

Solution on page 109

87

Mirror Land Chums

Rupert is surprised to see what his chums are wearing in Mirror Land. Can you draw them in their usual clothes in the frame below?

Which Story?

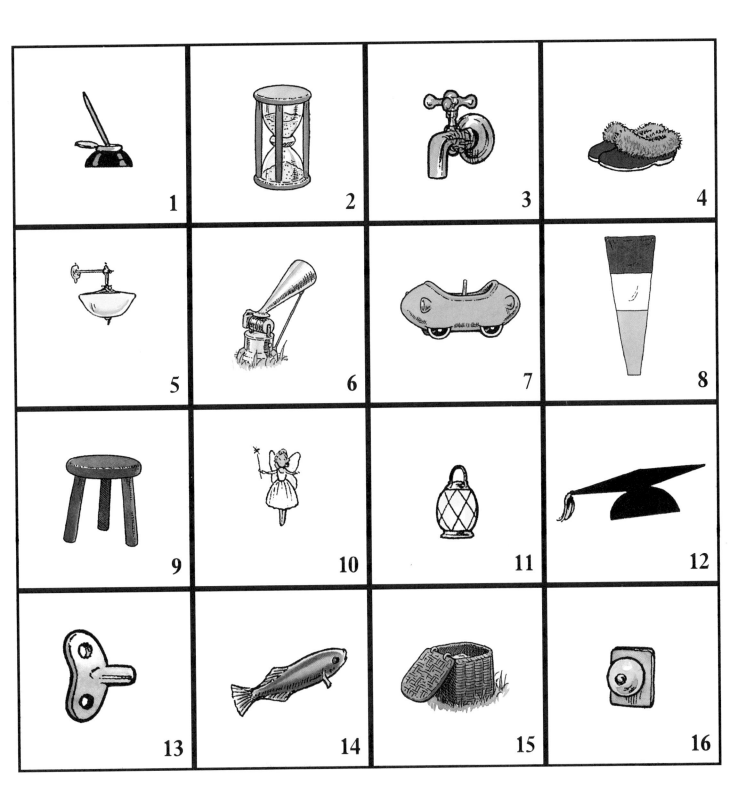

Each of the objects shown above appears in a story from this year's Annual.
Can you find where they are from?

Answers on page 109.

RUPERT and

It's nearly Christmas – time to go
Out carol singing in the snow . . .

It is nearly Christmas and Rupert is going carol singing with some of his friends. "Wrap up warm, dear," says his mother. "It's snowing outside!" "Deep and crisp and even!" chuckles Mr. Bear. "Just like the carol!" A few moments later, the doorbell rings, "It's Ottoline!" cries Rupert. "Hello!" she smiles. "I see you've got a lantern too. We'd better set off immediately so we don't keep Dr. Chimp and the others waiting . . ."

Santa's Present

*"Hello!" says Ottoline. "I see
You've got a lantern – just like me!"*

"I love the snow!" laughs Ottoline as the two pals hurry along. "Me too!" says Rupert. "If it keeps falling, there should be enough to build snowmen tomorrow." By the time the pair arrive, Dr. Chimp and the others are all ready to start. "Hello!" he calls. "I've made a list of the carols we're going to sing, starting with Silent Night. Algy Pug's brought his trumpet along, so if you forget the tune just listen to him."

*"More snow!" says Ottoline. "What fun!
We'll light the way for everyone!"*

*"Hello!" says Dr. Chimp. "You're all
Here now – so let's make our first call . . ."*

RUPERT GOES CAROL SINGING

"Well done!" Mr. Anteater cheers.
"The best singing I've heard for years!"

When Mrs. Sheep hears them begin,
She's so delighted she joins in!

"This way now everybody, our
Last call's the old Professor's tower!"

The pals start. Rupert rings the bell,
Then sings King Wenceslas as well . . .

Everyone in Nutwood looks forward to the carol singers and comes hurrying out to greet them as soon as they appear. "Well done!" chuckles Mr. Anteater. "Reminds me of when I was a youngster. Before your time, Dr. Chimp, but we sang carols even then, you know!" "Lovely!" smiles Mrs. Sheep, joining in the last verse. "Can I ask you all in for a mince pie and tea?" "That's very kind," says Dr. Chimp, "but we can't stop yet. There are a few more houses left to visit . . ."

At last, the carol singers have visited almost everyone in Nutwood. "Just one more call before we go home," declares Dr. Chimp and leads the way across the snow to the old Professor's tower . . . "Good King Wenceslas!" he whispers. "Sing up, everyone. As loud as you can!" "Happy Christmas!" calls Rupert, tugging the bell-pull as the others begin. "The Professor's bound to ask us in," he thinks. "Last year we had tea in his study, while Bodkin cut a special cake."

RUPERT IS PUZZLED

The music ends, but no-one comes
To greet the disappointed chums!

"How strange!" thinks Rupert. "Not a light
Is burning in the tower tonight . . ."

Next morning, he goes back to see
If he can solve the mystery.

He rings the bell but the front door
Stays shut, just as it did before . . .

To Rupert's surprise, the carol ends and nobody comes to the door . . . "Perhaps he didn't hear us?" says Gregory. "Impossible!" says Algy. "He must have gone away for Christmas." "What a pity!" says Dr. Chimp. "Oh well, we'd better be getting home. Thank you all for singing so well, and thank you, Algy, for playing the trumpet!" "I wonder if the Professor has really gone away?" thinks Rupert. He glances back towards the tower but all the windows are dark and nobody stirs.

Next morning, Rupert decides to go back to the Professor's tower to see if there is any sign of his old friend. In the daylight everything looks much more welcoming, with the Professor's flag fluttering in the breeze to let everyone know he's there. When he reaches the tower, Rupert pulls the bell as hard as he can. He hears it ring inside, but nobody comes to the door. "I wonder what's wrong?" he thinks. "I'd better try again, to make sure they know I'm here . . ."

RUPERT FINDS A STRANGE MIRROR

He tries the door. To his surprise
It isn't locked. "Hello!" he cries.

"Where can the old Professor be?
I'll look in the laboratory . . ."

"A mirror – with a strange machine!
It isn't one I've ever seen . . ."

"Astonishing! My hand can pass
Straight through this sheet of solid glass!"

As he waits for a reply, Rupert pushes at the door, only to find that it swings open straightaway. "Hello!" he calls. "Is anybody there?" No one replies as Rupert steps inside. "The Professor's probably hard at work," he thinks. "The door must open automatically." Making his way to the Professor's laboratory, he spots a strange new machine, set in front of a large mirror. "It's still switched on," he blinks. "The Professor can't have gone very far . . ."

Fascinated by the Professor's laboratory, Rupert can't resist taking a closer look at his latest invention. "How odd!" he gasps. "It looks like a mirror, but I can't see my reflection!" The longer he peers at it, the stranger it seems. "It's like a giant window," Rupert murmurs and reaches out to tap the glass. To his astonishment, his hand passes straight through without meeting any resistance. "Goodness!" he gasps. "It isn't a window either!"

*He steps right through the glass but then
Emerges in the lab again!*

*"It felt just like an empty frame,
But nothing this side looks the same!"*

*Then Bodkin suddenly appears.
"I've found you at last!" Rupert cheers.*

*"No visitors! My master's too
Important to see scamps like you!"*

Stepping forward, Rupert passes straight through the mirror and finds himself back in the laboratory, exactly where he started . . . "Just like an empty frame!" he thinks, then suddenly notices that everything looks strange. "That's not the Professor's machine!" he gasps. "It's smaller and a different shape. Nothing's the same!" he thinks. "I wonder where I am?" Just then he hears voices outside and somebody walking towards the door. "Who's there?" a voice calls angrily . . .

"Bodkin!" cries Rupert. "Thank goodness it's you. I was beginning to think . . ." "What are you doing here?" snaps the little servant. "The Professor doesn't allow strangers in his laboratory. He's hard at work and left strict instructions not to be disturbed . . ." "Strangers?" gasps Rupert. "But we're friends . . ." "Friends?" scoffs the servant. "Why should the Professor be friends with an urchin like you? Be off this instant, before I call a policeman and report you for trespassing!"

RUPERT SPOTS HIS PALS

"There's something else wrong!" Rupert thinks.
"The snow's all disappeared!" he blinks.

Then Rupert hears a distant call
And spots his chums, all playing ball.

He runs towards them, glad to see
That they're still acting normally . . .

But, as he joins them, they all say
They thought he'd gone on holiday!

Astonished by Bodkin's outburst, Rupert is even more surprised as he turns to leave the Professor's tower. "The snow!" he gasps. "It's disappeared . . ." Everywhere Rupert looks, brightly-coloured flowers are in full bloom, while the sun shines down as if it were a summer's day. "W . . . what's happened?" he asks, then catches sight of a group of chums, playing football on the Common. "I wonder if they've noticed how hot it's suddenly become . . ?"

When Rupert joins his pals, they all seem startled to see him. "Hello Trepur, what are you doing here?" cries Algy. "I thought you'd gone on holiday!" "No," says Rupert. "We never go away at Christmas . . ." "I thought you'd gone too!" shrugs Willie Mouse. "Never mind. Why don't you come and join the game?" "Thanks!" says Rupert. "But there's something I wanted to ask you . . ." "What's that?" says Bill. "I . . . I say!" gasps Rupert. "You're all wearing different clothes."

When Rupert tells them where he's been
They say its Nikdob he's just seen . . .

"Forget about him! Join the fun.
He's always cross with everyone!"

The game ends. All the pals have brought
A Christmas present of some sort . . .

"For Santa Claus!" says Bill. "We leave
Him presents every Christmas Eve!"

"Different clothes?" laughs Willie. "But this is what I always wear! What did you want to know?" "The . . . the Professor," stammers Rupert. "I went to see him, but Bodkin wouldn't let me in!" "Nikdob, you mean," cry the pals. "You should have known better to ask him! He's always so cross . . . The Professor's just as grumpy. He claims that visitors interrupt his work!" "Come on!" cries Willie, kicking the ball. Rupert joins in but still feels puzzled. Why is everything so strange?

As soon as the game is over, the pals tell Rupert they've got some Christmas presents for Santa . . . "What a good idea!" he cries. "I don't expect anyone has ever given *him* a present before." "But that's what we do every year!" blinks Algy. "Come on!" calls Bill. "Let's go to look for the sleigh. It should be waiting by the edge of the Common . . ." Sure enough, Rupert soon spots Santa's sleigh, with one of his helpers loading presents into a sack . . .

RUPERT RIDES IN THE SLEIGH

*"Thanks!" Santa's helper smiles as they
All load their gifts aboard the sleigh.*

*"I've brought Santa a present too . . .
Please can I take it back with you?"*

*"Yes," says the helper. "In you hop!
We're off now. This is our last stop."*

*"I'll ask Santa and see if he
Knows where the Professor can be . . ."*

"Thank you!" says the little man as he accepts the chums' gifts. "It was very kind of you to write and ask Santa what he wanted this year . . ." "How odd!" thinks Rupert. "Everything seems to be back to front!" "Have you brought anything?" asks Algy. "No," begins Rupert, then he suddenly has an idea. "Santa must get jolly cold at the North Pole," he tells the helper. "I'd like to give him a warm scarf. Can I come with you and deliver it myself?"

The little helper thinks hard for a moment, then gives a broad smile. "Of course you can come," he tells Rupert. "Hop aboard and I'll take you with me!" As soon as Rupert is ready, the reindeer bound forward and Santa's sleigh takes off. "Goodbye!" call the chums, all waving excitedly. As the sleigh rises high above Nutwood, Rupert spots the old Professor's tower. "That's where the mystery began," he murmurs. "Perhaps Santa will be able to tell me what's happened . . ."

RUPERT VISITS SANTA'S CASTLE

"There's Santa's castle, drawing near,
But what if he's changed too? Oh, dear!"

The sleigh arrives. "Can Rupert please
See Santa?" "Yes," a guard agrees.

As soon as Santa sees who's there
He smiles. "Bless me! It's Rupert Bear!"

"But you're from Nutwood! Tell me how
You managed to arrive just now . . ."

On and on speeds Santa's sleigh, over forests and mountains, until Nutwood has been left far behind. The little helper calls to the reindeer which soar even higher, up through the clouds. "There's Santa's castle!" cries Rupert. "I hope it hasn't changed too . . ." Landing in the castle courtyard, the helper leads Rupert to the main gate. "A visitor for Santa!" he tells one of the guards. "Please can I see him?" asks Rupert. "I know he's very busy, but there's something I need to ask . . ."

"Follow me!" calls the sentry and leads Rupert up a flight of steps to Santa's study. "Visitor, sir!" he calls. "Visitor?" asks Santa. "Why, it's Rupert Bear, from Nutwood . . ." "That's right!" smiles Rupert. "At least, I *think* it's Nutwood I came from. Everything there seems so different, I'm not really sure . . ." How did you get here?" asks Santa. "On the sleigh, with all your presents," explains Rupert. "**My** presents?" gasps Santa. "But they're not from Nutwood at all!"

"Ah!" Santa cries. "I understand!
You've travelled here from Mirror Land!"

"It's Nutwood – but the wrong way round!
Hence all the changes that you found . . ."

"From what you say, it seems to me
That's where the Professor must be!"

The pair fly off in Santa's sleigh
To Mirror Land, without delay . . .

"People in Nutwood don't send me presents!" explains Santa. "They're from Mirror Land . . ." "Mirror Land?" gasps Rupert. "The opposite to everything you know!" laughs Santa. "It looks like Nutwood but everything's different because it's on the wrong side of the mirror." "The Professor!" cries Rupert. "That must be why he's disappeared. His new machine took him to Mirror Land – and he hasn't come back!" "Goodness!" blinks Santa. "We'd better go and find him . . ."

As Santa leads the way to the courtyard, Rupert tells him all about the Professor's disappearance and how he found a strange mirror in the empty laboratory . . . "A doorway to Mirror Land!" cries Santa. "Then that's where we'll find him!" Climbing aboard the sleigh, he calls to his reindeer, who gallop up into the sky. "Hold tight!" he warns Rupert as they soar over the castle ramparts. "I've told my reindeer to take us back to Mirror Land as quickly as they can."

RUPERT SPOTS A LIGHT

They reach the tower as darkness falls.
"A light's been switched on!" Rupert calls.

"That's Nikdob's master! Never fear!
No-one will see us land up here . . ."

"This way!" says Santa. "In we go!
We'll search the tower from top to toe . . ."

"Stay close to me! Don't lag behind.
And not a sound of any kind!"

It is dark by the time Rupert and Santa reach their destination, with the stars twinkling in the sky and only the moon to light their way . . . "Look!" whispers Rupert as they near the tower, "There's a light on in the window!" "Somebody's still awake," says Santa. "But I don't suppose they're expecting any visitors . . ." Pulling gently on the reins, he lands silently on the roof. "Well done," he whispers to the reindeer. "Now we'll see if the Professor's still inside . . ."

Rupert follows Santa, but hesitates as he reaches the little door at the top of the tower. "What about Nikdob?" he asks. "He isn't very friendly . . ." "Of course not!" laughs Santa. "He's the exact opposite of the Professor's servant, Bodkin. One is pleasant and welcoming, while the other's bad-tempered and surly. Don't worry," he adds. "We can look for the Professor without Nikdob or his master ever knowing . . ." "How?" blinks Rupert, but Santa is already climbing down the winding steps.

Rupert and Santa's Present

RUPERT SEES NIKDOB'S MASTER

*"There's Nikdob and his master now!
We'll have to both get past somehow . . ."*

*"My sleeping powder!" Santa cries.
"Stand still, Rupert – and shut your eyes!"*

*The magic dust swirls through the air
And bright stars shimmer everywhere . . .*

*"Good!" Santa smiles. "Those two won't wake –
No matter how much noise we make!"*

Rupert and Santa tip-toe along a gloomy corridor until they spot Nikdob and his master, sitting by the fire. "He's just like the Professor!" gasps Rupert. "Almost," nods Santa, but he'd be just as cross as Nikdob if he knew we were here." Reaching deep into his pocket, the old man brings out a small sack and tells Rupert to cover his eyes. "I'm going to make sure they don't disturb us!" he whispers. "If we're to find the Professor we need to be able to search the whole tower."

As Rupert shuts his eyes, Santa opens the sack and sprinkles a handful of powder into the room. "Sleepy-dust!" he declares. "It's what I use to make sure children are fast asleep when I come to deliver their presents." Sure enough, when Rupert peers into the room, Bodkin and his master are sound asleep, surrounded by shimmering stars. "If you hadn't closed your eyes, you'd be sleeping too!" chuckles Santa. Leaving the pair to snooze by the fire, he sets off to begin the search . . .

102

RUPERT FREES THE PROFESSOR

"Professor!" the pair start to call
But nobody replies at all . . .

Then Rupert spots some steps that go
Down to the basement, far below . . .

He clambers down and hears a shout –
"How dare you? Come and let us out!"

"The Professor!" he turns a key
And sets the missing couple free!

Rupert and Santa search the tower for signs of the old Professor. "Hello!" calls Santa. "Is anybody there?" No one answers and every room they try is completely empty. "Perhaps he's not here after all?" suggests Santa. "He might have left the tower and gone off to explore." "Perhaps," agrees Rupert, then he spots a narrow flight of steps leading to the basement. "I wonder?" he murmurs. "If he was down there, he might not be able to hear us call . . ."

At the bottom of the stairs, Rupert and Santa find a cellar with a heavy wooden door . . . "Let me out this instant!" cries an angry voice. "I can't believe I'm being held a prisoner in my own home . . ." "The Professor!" smiles Rupert and reaches for the cellar key. As the door swings open, he sees Bodkin and his old friend, who are both delighted to be set free. "Thank goodness!" sighs the Professor. "For a moment, I thought you were those rascals who locked us up . . ."

RUPERT HEARS WHAT HAPPENED

*As Rupert greets the happy pair
They're both amazed that Santa's there . . .*

*"Our journey into Mirror Land
Just didn't go the way I'd planned . . ."*

*"Nikdob told my reflection he
Should lock us up immediately!"*

*"If their machine is like mine, then
It might send us all back again!"*

As they leave the cellar, Bodkin and the Professor are astonished to see Santa waiting outside . . . "Hello!" he smiles. "Rupert guessed you might be here, but however did you get into Mirror Land?" "A foolish experiment!" sighs the Professor. "The idea was so fascinating that I never stopped to think what it would be like to meet your own reflection. As soon as the machine was working, Bodkin and I simply stepped through the mirror to find out what lay on the other side . . ."

Explaining how he arrived in Mirror Land, the Professor tells Rupert that he and Bodkin came face to face with their doubles . . . "What a disaster!" he groans. "They weren't at all pleased to see us. Nikdob thought we must be impostors and convinced his master that we'd come to steal his machine!" As soon as he hears that the pair are sound asleep, the Professor is anxious to get back to the laboratory. "If I can reverse the machine, it might take us back to Nutwood!" he declares.

"Oh, dear! They've got the whole thing wrong –
To make it work would take too long . . ."

"Good!" Santa smiles. "Then they'll both stay
On their side while we get away . . ."

"We'll leave them here to slumber on –
They won't wake up until we've gone!"

"Climb in my sleigh. I'll show you how
To get back into Nutwood now . . ."

As soon as they reach the laboratory, the old Professor hurries over to inspect the mirror machine. "Oh dear!" he sighs. "This isn't the same as mine at all! I'm afraid it will never take us back to Nutwood . . ." "Good!" laughs Santa. "Then Nikdob and his master won't be able to follow you there . . ." "But how will we get home?" asks Rupert. "Don't worry," smiles Santa. "There's another way out of Mirror Land. Follow me, everyone!"

At the top of the tower, Rupert and the Professor find Nikdob and his master still slumbering by the fire. "When they wake up the whole thing will seem like a dream!" chuckles Santa. "It serves them right for trying to lock you up!" Leading the way to the roof, he points towards his sleigh. "One more flight and you'll all be back in Nutwood . . ." "Fancy that!" marvels Bodkin. "I once heard sleigh bells on Christmas Eve, but I never dreamt I'd ride in Santa's sleigh . . ."

RUPERT RETURNS TO NUTWOOD

The reindeer begin to fly
At full speed through the starry sky.

"Look!" Rupert gasps. "They're heading for
A massive archway – like a door!"

Thick fleecy cloud surrounds the sleigh
Then clears as it speeds on its way.

"We're back!" cries Rupert happily.
*This time it's **Nutwood** I can see . . ."*

The moment everyone is safely aboard, Santa calls to his reindeer, who soar up into the night sky . . . "Astounding!" gasps the Professor. "I'd no idea that reindeer could fly so fast!" Ahead of them Rupert spots a vast archway, set on a shimmering cloud. "It looks like a giant mirror!" he blinks. "Exactly!" chuckles Santa as the reindeer fly towards it and disappear from sight. "We're leaving Mirror Land behind us now and passing through a gateway to the *real* Nutwood . . ."

As Santa's sleigh plunges through the archway it is engulfed in a dense, white cloud . . . "Onward!" he cries to the reindeer until they suddenly emerge into brilliant sunshine. "We're back in Nutwood!" cries Rupert. "I can see the whole village spread out below – and everywhere's covered in snow . . ." "Just as you left it!" nods Santa. "All that remains now is to take you back to the Professor's tower." "Hurrah!" cheers Bodkin as they swoop towards it. "We're home at last!"

RUPERT SAYS GOODBYE

*"Goodbye!" calls Santa. "I must go!
It's Christmas Eve tonight, you know!"*

*The Professor tells Rupert how
He'll dismantle the machine now . . .*

*The pair thank Rupert once again –
"Thank goodness that you found us then!"*

*As Rupert hurries home he comes
Across a small group of his chums . . .*

As soon as he has set down his passengers, Santa takes off once more, to fly to his castle. "Goodbye!" calls Rupert. "And thank you for bringing us home . . ." Inside the tower, everything is exactly as it was before the journey began. "I don't think we'll be needing this again!" says Bodkin, covering up the mirror machine. "Certainly not!" agrees the Professor. "Enough of meddling with reflections! From now on, I intend to leave Mirror Land to Nikdob and his master!"

Now the mystery has been solved, Rupert decides it is time that he was getting home. "I must have been away for ages!" he gasps. "Thank you for all your help!" calls his friend. "If you hadn't come to look for us, Bodkin and I might still be stranded in Mirror Land . . ." Crossing the Common, Rupert spots a group of chums playing in the snow. "This time it's really them!" he laughs delightedly and hurries over to tell his pals all about his strange adventure . . .

RUPERT OPENS HIS PRESENTS

He tells them where he's been, but they
Just won't believe he's been away!

His parents hear his tale and seem
To think the whole thing's been a dream . . .

Next morning, Rupert wakes to find
The presents Santa's left behind.

"My scarf!" he laughs delightedly.
"Now Santa's given it to **me***!"*

"Hello!" calls Rupert as he joins the others. "You'll never guess where I've been!" To his dismay, none of them seem to believe his story. "Really!" laughs Bill. "You're having us on! You can't possibly have done all that – it's not even lunchtime yet . . ." When he gets home, Rupert's parents don't believe in Mirror Land either. "You must have been dreaming!" smiles his father. "Perhaps I was," thinks Rupert as he hangs up his Christmas stocking. "It does seem strange . . ."

Next morning, Rupert wakes to find a stocking full of wonderful presents at the foot of his bed . . . "Santa's been!" he cries and starts to unwrap them excitedly. Along with all the other gifts, he is intrigued to find a small, flat parcel with something soft inside . . . "My scarf!" he laughs as he tears it open. "The one I gave to Santa! So I *did* go to Mirror Land after all. It wasn't just a dream . . ."

THE END

Follow Rupert every day

in the Express

John Harrold.

ANSWERS TO PUZZLES:

(P.84) WHERE IS GREGORY?:
CHALKTOWN

(P.86) SPOT THE DIFFERENCE:
1) Tin missing, top shelf; 2) Label missing from jar; 3) Button missing, Mr. Chimp's shirt; 4) Mrs. Badger's hat missing; 5) Stalk missing from pumpkin; 6) Eggs missing from bowl behind Mr. Chimp; 7) Bill's bowtie missing; 8) Top hoop missing from apple barrel; 9) Door handle missing; 10) Door has no window.

(P.87) CROSSWORD:

Across	Down
4. Inspector	1. Mirror
5. Scarf	2. Podgy
7. Pompey	3. Binnacle
9. Skates	6. Horace
10. Quarry	8. Chalk
12. Bill	11. Whale
13. Beachcombers	12. Bodkin
16. Hedgehog	13. Baths
17. Presents	14. Songs
18. Reindeer	15. Wise Old Owl
25. Nutwood	17. Property
26. Tigerlily	19. Elves
27. Lion	20. Hot water
	21. Turtle
	22. Autumn
	23. Carols
	24. Chimp

(P.89) WHICH STORY?:
(1) P. 30; (2) P. 59; (3) P. 75;
(4) P. 8; (5) P. 74; (6) P. 11;
(7) P. 76; (8) P. 48; (9) P. 95;
(10) P. 90; (11) P. 91; (12) P. 30;
(13) P. 15; (14) P. 82; (15) P. 82;
(16) P. 95.